INDIGO ICE

A POST-APOCALYPTIC NOVEL

KELLEE L. GREENE

This is a work of fiction. Names, characters, organizations, places, events and incidents are either products of the author's imagination or are used fictitiously. Any resemblance to actual persons, living or dead, events or locales is entirely coincidental.

Copyright © 2018 Kellee L. Greene

First Edition January 2019

BOOKS BY KELLEE L. GREENE

Red Sky Series

Red Sky - Book 1

Blue Cloud - Book 2

Black Rain - Book 3

White Dust - Book 4

Indigo Ice - Book 5

Book 6 Coming Soon!

Ravaged Land Series

Ravaged Land - Book 1

Finding Home - Book 2

Crashing Down - Book 3

Running Away - Book 4

Escaping Fear - Book 5

Fighting Back - Book 6

Ravaged Land: Divided Series

The Last Disaster - Book 1

The Last Remnants - Book 2

The Last Struggle - Book 3

Falling Darkness Series

Unholy - Book 1

Uprising - Book 2

Hunted - Book 3

The Island Series

The Island - Book 1

The Fight - Book 2

The Escape - Book 3

The Erased - Book 4

The Alien Invasion Series

The Landing - Book 1

The Aftermath - Book 2

Destined Realms Series

Destined - Book 1

ONE

Knowing what time it was, wasn't something that was easy since the world ended. By my best guess, I figured we'd been traveling for about a month since leaving behind the town filled with the criminally insane.

It was just the four of us now, and even though Nick had been injured long ago, he moved quickly. It could have been that he had healed more or it could have been that he refused to slow down until we were somewhere he felt safe.

I found it hard to believe that we'd ever find somewhere that was truly safe, but it wasn't like we had a lot of options. We had to stop somewhere or keep walking forever.

So much time had gone by, and still, we didn't

know what was going on. Before we'd lost power, the talking head on TV had said it was some kind of attack. It hadn't only been one attack, it had just been the first. Whoever was doing this was relentless. It was just one after the other with no end in sight.

They were unusual. Terrorizing. And devastating attacks.

We were lucky to be alive. If it could be called luck.

It didn't matter how far we walked away from White and his pal Ripley who'd been in charge of the little town. There wasn't any distance that would make it feel like we were far enough away.

"We should find somewhere to stop soon," Bronx said looking up toward the darkening sky. It was a sparkling blue, but at the horizon, it was turning a darker navy shade. The shadows were growing, and I hated this time of night because I always felt like we were being followed, although, sometimes it felt like they were ghosts behind us, haunting us.

"I've been looking for the last six miles, but there hasn't been anything," Nick said.

"There was that shed," Molly said with a shrug.

Nick placed his hand on her shoulder and

rubbed it as if he were trying to provide her warmth. "We can do better than a shed, don't you think?"

"I hope so," she said grinning at him with hearts in her eyes.

I bit my cheek so I wouldn't sigh my annoyance, but there wasn't anything I could do to stop my eyes from rolling in almost a complete circle.

We'd been surviving on what we'd been able to find along the way. There was still plenty of supplies left behind in the small towns and houses we came upon.

Food and water were abundant because so much of the population had been eliminated. Nick worried it wouldn't always be that way. We needed to take advantage of it while we could which is why we were searching for a place to stay.

Our plan was to find a secluded place and make it our base. We'd have food, water, anything we'd need, we'd stock. How we'd defend it, I didn't know, but I was sure Nick had ideas.

There hadn't been any more attacks since the last. I hoped that the white dust would be the last one, but it probably wasn't.

Whoever was trying to eliminate the population wasn't going to give up until every last soul was gone. Then again, for all I knew, they were just testing their weapons for the future. Maybe they already were happy with the number of people they'd killed.

It was frustrating not knowing who had launched the attacks, but there was no way we could know. There was no communication whatsoever and everyone we came across was in the same situation we were... lost.

Something rustled in a nearby bush and I jumped back. My hands clenched into tight fists.

Bronx looked at me as a bunny hopped out in front of us. "Just a bunny."

"Those things might be diseased or rabid or something," I said.

"Are you going to punch the rabid out of them?" Bronx asked raising his brow as he smirked at me.

"Cute, really cute," I said shaking my head.

His eyelids lowered ever-so-slightly. "Thank you. So are you."

Things had been great between Bronx and I. Having him in my life gave me a reason to try. To be better. To be tougher.

But there was something terrible that came along with our relationship and that was that I didn't know how I could survive if I lost him. One night we'd been talking and he made me promise that I would keep trying. He made me promise to never give up no matter what.

I couldn't make the promise to him, at least, not right away. But after I did, I made him promise the same.

I wasn't sure it would be possible to go on if anything happened to him. What would I have left? A promise is a promise though, right? I tried to convince myself ever since I'd uttered the words that I hadn't lied to him, but I worried that I was just lying to myself too.

"Are there any bars left?" Molly asked pulling on the backpack I had slung over my right shoulder.

"Yeah," I said sliding the pack off and handing it to her. She could carry the heavy pack for a while, my shoulder needed a break.

We'd stuffed the pack as full as we could when we'd found it, adding more and more until it looked like the zipper was going to pop. It was a touch lighter since we'd first filled it, but I'd been carrying it all day. I felt like if I had to have the weight any longer, I was going to develop a hunchback.

Molly groaned but took the backpack from me. She took several quick steps until she caught back up with Nick and offered him a bar. He smiled at her as he took it from her and sucked it down in two bites.

Nick stopped and pointed to something near the horizon. "Check that out."

I blinked several times and squinted. There was a long, cracked driveway that twisted and turned all the way up a hill. At the top of that hill sat a mansion.

"Looks like the place I always dreamed of having one day," Molly said smiling and shaking her head as if she'd entered a dreamland. After a quick moment, her shoulders slumped as she remembered everything she'd been through and what had become of our world.

"Should we check it out?" Nick asked, glancing at Bronx and then at me.

I shrugged. "Seems big. A lot of space to worry about checking over."

"Yeah, Gwen's right," Bronx said.

"But we haven't seen a soul in weeks," Molly said. "Let's just have a peek even if we don't stay there."

"It's all right with me if it's all right with them," Nick said wrapping his arm around Molly's shoulders.

Bronx nudged me lightly with his elbow. "We might not be able to find anything else."

"I know, I know," I said releasing a heavy sigh.

"Well, then, what are we waiting for? Let's go check it out."

Molly practically squealed as she did a short little bunny hop. "I'm going to pretend it's mine. I'm also going to pretend it's in California rather than out here in the middle of nowhere."

"Some people like to have a house in the middle of nowhere," I said.

"I'm not one of those people," Molly said batting her thick eyelashes.

"Are you wearing mascara?" I asked.

Molly narrowed her eyes as if she were in a makeup commercial. "I'm worth it."

I rolled my eyes, but I couldn't stop a tiny laugh from seeping out from between my lips.

"Want to borrow some?" Molly said flicking her eyebrows up and down as she glanced quickly at Bronx.

I shook my head. "No thanks."

"Suit yourself," Molly said. "I'm going to do whatever I can so I don't have to look like an old maid even if everything around us is falling apart. If I have to go out, I'm going out looking my best."

"You're beautiful without makeup too," Nick said pulling her closer.

My stomach twisted. I still couldn't let go of

what happened with Blair. If Nick hadn't met Molly things would have been different. At least I think they would have. The burns and blisters from the white powder had damaged her skin severely. None of us knew what that stuff would have done to her long term.

It was weird but I missed Blair. Even though she and I hadn't really gotten along that well, everything felt different without her. She was supposed to be here with us.

I hated change. I'd always hated change.

Bronx and Nick both pulled out their guns as we approached the house. It was quiet. I felt like there were more eyes on me from our surroundings than there were from inside the house.

We walked around the front of the house looking in every window that we could. Most of the curtains were closed but several windows had a tiny space where we could see the beautifully decorated home that looked as though it hadn't ever been lived in.

"Looks empty," Nick said softly. "At least these few rooms do."

"Doesn't mean the whole house is," I muttered.

Bronx's eyes shot up toward the sky. "Unfortunately, we're out of time."

"Maybe we should hide in the garage," I suggested.

"The garage?" Molly frowned.

"It looked like a nice garage," I said with a quick shrug.

"I've been sleeping on floors, hiding in basements, and eating hay. We have this," Molly said gesturing at the house, "and you want me to sleep in a garage? No thanks. You guys go hide in there, but I'm sleeping in a bed tonight, and something tells me it's going to be divine."

Molly stomped around Nick and walked up to the front door. She turned the doorknob and pushed the door open.

"Jesus," Nick mumbled and quickly followed after her.

Bronx shrugged and looked over his shoulder at the area behind us. "Let's check it out, then we can go in the garage."

"Yippee," I said as he grabbed my hand and pulled me along.

We stepped inside and Bronx closed the door softly behind us. Molly was standing there her hands folded up near her chin as she slowly spun wearing a silly grin.

"This is amazing," she said.

I looked at the little table next to the door. It had a beautiful dish filled with dust-covered potpourri. The table had just as much dust if not more, only there were fingerprints near the edge.

I tapped Bronx on the shoulder. "Look at this."

"Huh," Bronx said. "Looks recent."

"The door was open," I said drawing in a breath as I looked at all the doorways and openings.

Bronx lowered his voice. "Hey Nick," he whispered. "I don't think we're alone here."

Nick gestured at an opened bottle of water next to a pistol sitting on a coffee table next to a fancy lamp that looked as though it had cost more than I had paid for my car.

"I don't think so either," Nick said slowly trying to move us back to the door.

We didn't make it more than a few steps before the stairs started creaking and a clean pair of sneakers stepped into view. Nick stood in front of Molly and me and moved his gun-holding hand behind his back.

The man was holding a roll of toilet paper in one hand and an open magazine in the other. He stopped about half-way down the stairs and looked at us.

"Um... hello," he said his eyes darted over toward

the table with the gun. I didn't think he was looking at his bottle of water.

The man took another step down, shifting his gaze toward us. He wasn't looking at his gun, but I knew all he was thinking about was getting to it.

Nick must have too because he raised up his gun. "That's far enough."

TWO

The man held up his hands without dropping the toilet paper or the magazine. "I—I don't want any trouble. Take whatever you want and leave."

"Wait," Molly said cocking her head to the side. "Do I know you from somewhere?"

The man wore a little smirk as he lowered his hands slightly. "You just might."

"Do you know me?" Molly said narrowing her eyes.

"No," he said squinting back at her. "Should I?"

"Oh. Wait. Yeah, yeah, I do know you," Molly said slapping her palm on her thigh. "You guys!" she said spinning to face us for a split second. "This is that one guy!"

"What one guy?" Nick asked scratching the side of his head. He stared at the guy, but I could tell he had no idea who he was and neither did I.

"You know! He's that one singer! From that band. Oh my God, you know!" Molly said pushing Nick's arm down as she gawked at the guy. "You are him, aren't you?"

The man took another step down with a swagger in his hips. He paused when Nick raised the gun up again. The man held up his hands again.

"Yeah, that's me," he said with a nervous chuckle. "That guy from that one band."

"I knew it! What are you doing out here?" Molly asked crossing her arms. She smiled at him as if he were an old friend.

"This is my second house. My home away from home," the man said. "Can I come down before I fall down the stairs? My balance isn't that great these days."

I wondered if his issues were from too much partying because it wasn't from old age. He didn't look like he could have been a day over twenty-five.

Nick nodded but he didn't bother to lower his gun. "I have no clue who you are."

I shook my head but maybe he did look a little familiar. He must have been from some band I

13

wasn't very familiar with because I couldn't place him. Based on the size of the house, he must have been quite popular and he definitely had the looks of a rock star.

"I'm Christian," He said offering us all a little wave. "I really don't want any trouble though. Feel free to take whatever you want, although I'd appreciate it if you left me a little something to get by on."

"We're not here to take your things," Molly said flapping her hand at him. "All we wanted was to find somewhere to stay for the night."

"How do I know you won't kill me in my sleep?" Christian asked with a nervous laugh. There was a curl to his lips but a seriousness in his eyes. I recognized it because I'd had the same feeling before myself.

It's that feeling you get when you have to be with someone you don't trust. In my case that person had ended up setting my grandma's house on fire and almost killed me. My gut instincts had been right, not that I was surprised.

Christian didn't need to worry about us though, but of course, he didn't know that. Nick wouldn't pull the trigger unless he didn't have a choice. All Christian had to do was avoid doing something stupid.

"We don't kill people," Nick said lowering his head slightly but keep his eyes on Christian. "Unless, of course, we have to."

"Well, you won't have to," Christian said.

"Yeah? Good. I'd hate to waste my ammo," Nick said tucking his gun back into the back of his waist-band. "Mind if I hold on to your gun while we're here?"

Christian's jaw tightened. "I'd rather you didn't. Nothing personal, it's just that I don't know you guys. Can't I put it in my waistband like you did all gangster-like?"

"I was a police officer. If I had my holster, I'd use it," Nick said.

"Well, if you say you were a cop, then it must be true," Christian said letting his eyebrows bob up and down.

A quick sigh burst out between Molly's lips. "Well, I know you are who you say you are. I think I bought every single one of your albums. Hell, my friends and I even saw you play out in Cali."

"I appreciate that," Christian said. "At least I think I do... I mean, it's all pretty meaningless now."

"You have this whole place to hide in until help arrives," Molly said. "Has anyone else come around?"

Christian shook his head. "Thankfully, no. You are the first strangers to wander up here. It gets pretty scary at night though. This big house makes a lot of noises."

"Maybe there have been people in here and you didn't even know it," Nick said. "They stayed in the east wing and your paths never crossed."

Christian shrugged. "Comforting thought. Doesn't matter though, I'm stuck here. I mean, it's not all bad. I have food, water, alcohol and a roof over my head. All I do is sit around and write music all day... music that no one will ever hear."

"I would love to hear it," Molly said practically swaying to the invisible notes.

"Really?" Christian asked. "Here let me show you guys around first. Then I can play my latest for you."

"That would be a dream come true," Molly said with hearts in her eyes.

Christian reached down and picked up his gun. He flipped it around and offered it to Nick. "If you're going to kill me, there isn't going to be much I can do about it anyway. Truth is, I have no idea how to use that thing. It was my bodyguards' gun... he...," Christian said his voice cracking, "didn't make it. I just carry it around in case I can scare someone off. That wasn't going to be happening with you guys."

"It would have worked better if you wouldn't have left it behind on the table. You should have been carrying it with you," Nick said with a small chuckle as he checked over the gun. He turned and offered it to me, but I shook my head.

Christian ran his finger through his wild, wavy hair as he looked me up and down. He turned back to Nick and the ends of his lips curled up slightly. "I wasn't really expecting company, so I thought it would be okay on that table. I don't even like touching that thing."

"There are some really evil guys out there. You're lucky it's us that found you and not them," Nick said.

"I wasn't even sure if there was anyone else alive, to be honest," Christian said with a shiver.

I hadn't noticed how cold the house had been until I saw his shoulders quiver. The small amount of sunlight that had been there before we came inside had probably diminished completely.

"Come with me," Christian said. "I'll show you around."

Molly clapped her hands and tried to muffle her

squeal of delight. "This place is like my dream house."

"It was mine too," Christian said. "Bought the land and had it custom built. Only owned it for a year before all this happened. Didn't even get to enjoy it."

"Wow," Molly said her voice thick with jealousy. "You know, I had just gotten my first major role before this shit went down. I was out here visiting my parents when the shit hit the fan."

"Cool," Christian said not sounding at all as if he cared. He gestured toward the door. "I'll show you where the kitchen is first."

We walked through Christian's enormous house. There were bedrooms and rooms with TV screens. A room with a bar. It didn't look as though any of the rooms had been used.

"This, in here, is the pantry," Christian said after showing us the massive kitchen. The shelving units were stacked from top to bottom with everything you could imagine. My mouth watered at all of the options that were available to us after weeks, maybe months of snacking on nothing but bars and granola. "Help yourself to anything you'd like. I have a gas stove that still works."

"Where have you been sleeping?" Molly asked.

She'd probably asked because none of the bedrooms looked as though they'd been used. Maybe Christian was the type that was tidy and made his bed every morning.

"I've been sleeping in my studio," Christian said jerking his chin to the side. "This way."

We followed him across the hallway and into the smallest room we'd seen on the tour, but still, by no means was it small. There were pillows on the sofa and more stacked on the floor.

He had several blankets strewn about and a pile of dirty dishes and wrappers scattered on top of his large wooden desk. Christian had been the opposite of tidy.

"Does the fireplace work?" Molly asked rubbing her palms together.

"It does," Christian said with a half-frown, "but I'm running out of wood."

"Lots of useable wood out there," Bronx said. "You have an axe?"

Christian shrugged. "Could be one in the garage. Anyway, I have enough for now. I'll worry about it when the time comes."

"Better to be prepared," Bronx said.

Nick shook his head. I was pretty sure I could read his mind at that moment and he was wondering how Christian had made it this long. Sadly, he could have thought the same thing about us.

"So, you said you wanted to stay for the night?" Christian asked.

"Well, that was before we knew it was occupied," Nick said.

"Nick," Molly groaned as she placed her hands on her hips. "It's dark out, it's not like we have a lot of options."

Nick gave her a small nod. "We can stay in the garage."

"That works," Christian said.

"Thanks," Nick said. "But I'm going to hang onto your gun until we leave."

Christian chuckled. "Like I told you before I really have no idea how to use it anyway. If I tried, I'd probably just end up shooting myself."

"Thanks for showing us around," Nick said. "Nice place you got here."

"Thanks," Christian said.

Bronx and I were already at the door to leave his studio, but Nick practically had to pull Molly out of the room.

"I bet the beds are so soft," Molly said. "And clean."

"I don't know about that," Christian said. "Maid

service hasn't come in some time. Dust builds up quickly."

Nick grabbed Molly's hand and pulled her back. She let out a long sigh.

"Look, you guys can stay inside," Christian said.

"Are you sure?" Molly said wiggling her hand free from Nick. She didn't wait for him to answer. "We really appreciate it. That's so kind of you."

"Yeah," Christian said. "I'm going to lock myself in here though. You guys are on your own."

Molly cocked her head to the side and scrunched up her nose. "Any other rooms with fireplaces?"

"A few," Christian said flopping down in his pile of blankets on the sofa. "Make yourself at home, I guess."

"Thanks," Molly said bobbing her head as she backed toward the door. "Thank you so much. How about that song?"

THREE

The room on the same side of the hallway opposite Christian's studio also had a fireplace. It was the room we opted to stay inside.

Nick was hesitant to stay so close to him, but when the warmth of the fire filled the room, he stopped mentioning his concerns.

We could hear him through the wall performing for Molly. It had looked as though he'd been slightly disappointed when we all hadn't stayed, but it hadn't stopped him from putting on a show.

"She shouldn't be in there alone with him," Nick said.

"What's he going to do sing her to death?" Bronx asked kicking his legs up on the coffee table.

The room had big comfy chairs, a large fluffy

sofa and a massive screen attached to the wall. I wondered if it had been a movie room and if it had ever been used. There was even a real popcorn maker behind a counter that was fully stocked with snacks, candy, and chocolates.

"He's singing me to death," Nick grumbled.

Bronx chuckled. "I think I heard this one on the radio. Sounds familiar, don't you think?"

Nick shook his head.

"I think I've heard it too," I said. I crossed my arms and looked at Nick sideways. "If I didn't know better, I'd say you sound jealous."

"I don't get jealous," Nick said sitting down for two seconds before popping back up and starting to pace. "Man, I just don't think we can trust this guy. Or this place for that matter. There are about a thousand ways to get inside and we wouldn't hear them until they were right up on us."

"Well," Bronx said with a growl as he stretched his arms over his head before folding them behind himself. He slouched down and stretched his legs out in front of him. "We're here for the night."

I couldn't take my eyes off of Bronx. If only we would have had our own room in this amazing house. I exhaled and forced myself to look away from him.

"We'll just take turns keeping watch like we

always have," I said. "It's just one night. We've probably stayed in places far more dangerous than this mansion."

The soft music coming from the other room stopped. Nick stopped pacing and stared at the wall. It was at least fifteen minutes before the music started up again and Nick began pacing again.

He stopped at the window and looked out between the blinds. I could see it was pitch black outside.

"I'll take the first watch," Nick said with a heavy exhale. "You two should get some rest."

Bronx patted the spot on the sofa next to him and raised a brow. I just shook my head and smiled at him but that didn't stop me from sitting down next to him.

"Get some rest," Bronx said placing a kiss on the top of my head.

"I'm not even a little tired," I said but it wasn't the truth. My mind wasn't tired but my body was beyond exhausted.

The music coming from the other room was soothing. It was weird hearing it... music was something I hadn't heard since the day the sky turned red.

Apparently, it was like magic because it lulled

me to sleep. And no one woke me before early morning.

Bronx was at the window with his head resting on his closed fist. Nick was on the floor with his mouth hanging open and Molly was curled up in the chair with a small smile on her face.

I must have been dead to the world because I couldn't even remember when Molly had come back into the room. She must have come back really late.

"Morning sunshine," Bronx whispered.

"Is it?" I asked.

"It is what?"

I yawned. "Morning."

"Will be soon," Bronx said. "Sun's touching the horizon."

I stood up and stretched before walking over to Bronx. He leaned back slightly as I wrapped my arms around him. I loved how warm he felt. Hell, I loved how warm the room felt with the fire going.

"Nick's going to want to get going soon," I said glancing over my shoulder at him. "How much sleep has he gotten?"

"A few hours," Bronx said.

"So, not enough." I frowned.

Bronx pushed his shoulders back. "Might be more than he's gotten over the last few weeks."

"Christian said we could stay longer if we wanted to," Molly said.

"I don't want to stay any longer," Nick said sucking in a deep breath as he pushed himself into a seated position.

"You both just sit there pretending to be asleep or what?" I asked feeling the tension in my brow.

Nick growled as he got to his feet. "No, you guys just talk too fricken loud. No consideration for anyone but yourselves. None."

I rolled my eyes. "Funny."

"We're not staying," Nick said turning to Molly.

"Nick," Molly said leaning forward. She was suddenly wide awake. "Just for a few—"

"No!" Nick had said the word so sharply we all jumped as if his word had been a bullet zipping through the room. He cleared his throat. "We need to get back out there. We're not going to waste any more time here."

"This isn't wasting time, Nick," Molly said puffing out her lower lip. "We're safe here. We have food. Staying here is being smart."

Nick's body stiffened. "This place is far from safe. Every minute we sit inside this place is a minute we could be out there finding our own place."

"There is so much food here," Molly said. "More than Christian will ever eat."

"Enough!" Nick said his lips barely moving.

Bronx stood and held out his palms. Concern filled his eyes as anger bubbled up inside Nick.

Whatever was going on with Nick was something far beyond jealousy.

"What's going on, Nick?" I asked as I crossed my arms. "We could stay another day. We all need the rest. You more than any of us."

And that's when it hit me. Nick was sleep deprived. There were dark circles under his eyes and his eyelids drooped downward. It was how he'd looked when he woke up after a night of binging, only out here I knew he hadn't been partaking in drugs or booze.

"We don't have the time to waste," Nick said his eyes bulging so wide I could see the red spiderwebs in the whites. He pointed at the window. "We need to be out there searching."

"What we all need is a break," Molly said shaking her head. "I can't keep up at this pace."

"Well, you're going to have to," Nick said.

Molly's lips pressed together. "Am I?" The floorboards creaked as she stomped her way to the door.

"You can do whatever the hell you want I suppose, but I'm" —she opened the door— "staying."

My muscles tightened when Molly slammed the door closed behind her. Nick looked like he was about to throw his fist into the wall. His shoulders bobbed up and down rapidly. He drew in a deep breath and his nostrils flared as his eyes met mine.

"We're leaving in ten!" Nick shouted at the door. He hit his thigh with his fist and muttered a curse.

I took a step toward him and opened my mouth.

Nick held up a finger and stared into my eyes. "Don't. Just, don't."

I froze in place. It felt like something was pushing my words back inside. I couldn't tell him that I thought he was making a mistake. Not necessarily a mistake with staying but a mistake with Molly.

After what happened with Blair, I didn't want to see him mess up again. I knew Nick wasn't any better at dealing with loss than I was.

Nick opened the door and hesitated for a moment before speaking in his usual tone. "I'm going to check out the kitchen."

FOUR

Nick hadn't been gone for more than ten minutes when there was a knock at the door. Molly hadn't come back but it had been her, she wouldn't have bothered to knock.

The door opened and Christian peeked his head inside. "Weird knocking on my own damn door. Can I talk to you guys for a minute?"

"Sure, come on in," Bronx said stuffing his hands into his pocket as he walked closer to the door. "Feels pretty weird inviting you into a room in your house."

Christian chuckled.

"What did you want to talk about?" Bronx asked as I sat down and looked out of the window.

Everything outside was still as the sun started to illuminate the yard. It was so quiet that I was pretty sure if someone were walking toward the house, I would have heard them coming.

"Molly said you all declined my invitation to stay awhile?" Christian said.

"That's right," Bronx said. "Nick really wants to get back on the road."

"Molly is hell-bent on staying," Christian said. "Here's the thing though...," Christian swallowed. "I don't want to stay here. If it's all right with you guys, I'd like to tag along."

I shook my head. "You don't even know where we're going."

"I don't care where you're going," Christian said staring into my eyes. "You don't know what it's like out here. I'm alone. It's hard... it's really hard."

"Honestly, man, it's up to Nick," Bronx said.

"We're not a very trusting group," I added.

Christian smiled. "I picked up on that. Tempts me to ask what you all saw out there but maybe it's better that I don't know. Anyway, I gave the man my gun, what more could I do to prove that he can trust me?"

"There's probably nothing you can do," Bronx said with a half-shrug.

"I can't stay here alone another day," Christian said. He lowered his gaze. "I'm just a guy. I have no desire to hurt anyone or do anything that would get someone hurt."

"I believe that," Bronx said. "But it's a shitty world out there. You're probably safer here."

Christian ran both hands through his wild hair. "I don't care. I'm sick and tired of being safe. It wasn't like I was ever safe before... being safe is killing me slowly." Christian took a step forward. "I'd rather go out there and face getting killed fast."

"Nick's in the kitchen," I said with a short sigh. "It's him you're going to have to convince."

"All right," Christian said.

"I should probably warn you," I said.

Christian cocked his head to the side. "Warn me about what?"

"Nick's in a terrible mood," I said.

"That guy seems like someone that's in a bad mood a lot," Christian muttered before flashing us a small wave and stepping out of the door.

Bronx walked over to me and placed his hand on my shoulder. "Think that was a good idea sending him to Nick?"

"Probably not but if he can't handle Nick in one of his moods, he should know that now," I said grinning to myself. "Maybe it'll change his mind about heading out of this place."

"You think he should stay?" Bronx asked.

"I don't think this place is all that bad."

The door behind us opened and we both turned to see Molly step inside the room. She didn't bother to close the door behind her. "It's not bad. This place is amazing. Nick is being stubborn and foolish."

"He's just trying to look out for us. He's trying to do the right thing," I said.

"By making us go out there where there is nothing but poison and evil?" Molly said flopping down on the chair and crossing her arms. "It's good here. It can be great here."

Bronx looked at me before sitting down on the sofa. He leaned forward, resting his elbows on his knees.

"Do you know that Christian wants to leave with us?" Bronx asked.

Molly looked away. "He may have mentioned something, but he... he's willing to wait a few days... for us to rest up." She turned back to Bronx with tears welling up in her eyes. "I can't keep pushing forward like this. I'll stay here alone if I have to. This is about four million times better than hiding in a closet."

"You should be telling this to Nick," I said.

Molly laughed although she didn't seem to find

anything actually to be funny. "Waste of my breath. Much like right now."

"Sorry," I said because it was true. She was wasting her breath. There wasn't anything Bronx or I could do to help her. Molly was going to have to work it out with Nick.

"Where is he anyway?" Molly asked.

"Kitchen," Bronx said. "Christian went to talk to him."

Molly stood up. "Oh, I'm not sure that's a good idea."

"Why not?" I asked cocking my head to the side.

"No reason, I guess. I just know Nick and I don't really see those two getting along," Molly said pressing her fingers to her temples. "Then again I'm a terrible judge of character. I'm still not sure I know anything about Nick."

"Me either," I muttered.

She eyed me quickly before chewing on a fingernail. "It's sad when I think I know Christian better than him and I've known him less than twenty-four hours. Unless, of course, you count all the hours of listening to his music and swooning over his music videos."

"That doesn't count," Bronx said.

Molly flapped her hand at him. "I know that, of

course. Dammit, I should go find them. Make sure Nick hasn't killed Christian."

"I don't get it," I said shaking my head. "Why would he kill Christian?"

"Christian didn't know that Nick and I are kind of a... I don't know what... a thing," Molly said biting her lip.

"Jesus," I said swallowing down the bubbles that came up the back of my throat. What had she done?

Molly rolled her eyes. "Don't give me that look. He just made a small pass at me. I told him I was with Nick. It's all good."

"Drama, drama, drama," I said.

"I was an actress," Molly said blinking several times. "Anyway, I'm going to go find him."

Molly stopped before she got far. I could hear the chuckles echoing in the hallway. It sounded as if Nick and Christian were actually getting along.

"What's this all about?" I asked as they stepped inside the room.

Nick smacked Christian on the back. "The two of us got to talking. That's all."

"Talking about what?" Molly asked looking like she was about to be sick. I wondered how far that pass had gotten before Molly had shot Christian down.

"Christian and I came up with a plan," Nick said with a small smirk.

I narrowed my eyes at him. Something was different about Nick. "You came up with a plan? You said we were leaving in ten minutes, that was the plan. Now you come in here all smiles with a new plan? What's going on Nick?"

"Christian and I got off on the wrong foot," Nick said leaning against the wall. "He's not any different than we are. He needs our help, so we'll help him."

Bronx and I exchanged a glance.

"So, what's your plan?" Bronx asked.

"We're going to stay another night. We'll pack things up, take a bath, and in the morning, we'll head out," Nick said.

"And I'll be joining you," Christian said with a curl to his lips that nearly matched Nick's. Christian looked at Molly. "Everyone's happy."

I studied Nick but he wouldn't look my way. "What changed your mind?"

"I changed my mind," Nick said. "Christian said no one has come this way. I realized I was being hasty."

"You? Hasty? I don't believe it," I teased.

"My sister, the joker," Nick said pointing his finger in my direction.

Christian's eyes narrowed. "Sister, huh? How nice for you two. I'm sure none of my family is out there. Even if they were, I'm probably the last person they'd want to see."

I wanted to tell Christian that Nick had been the last person I wanted to see, too, but it had, for the most part, worked out. In fact, things had been good between us until the whole Blair thing.

I still blamed him. And I was pretty sure that deep down he blamed himself too. It was a good thing that we were far from drugs because he likely would have fallen back down into his hole of despair.

"So, what do we do now?" I asked.

"Take a bath, eat, sleep, whatever you want to do," Christian said.

"A bath?" I asked.

Nick nodded. "We need to use what's left of the water since we can't carry it all. There are jugs and jugs in storage."

"A bath," I said the word as if it were foreign.

"I'll show you," Christian said.

"Umm, sure," I said glancing at Bronx over my shoulder. He gave me a little nod and I walked over to Christian.

Nick crossed his arms and turned to Molly. "And we need to talk."

"Okay," Molly said placing her hand on her stomach. She followed him out of the room. I could hear their steps as they walked down the hallway and into one of the other rooms.

"Ready?" Christian asked.

"Sure," I said and followed him out of the room. We hadn't even made it more than halfway down the long hallway before a door popped open behind us and Molly burst out with tears streaming down her face.

I stopped and sighed. "I should probably go talk to her."

"No need," Christian said as he spun me back around toward the kitchen. I placed my hand on his chest to catch myself before slamming into him.

"I really think I should," I said swallowing hard as I took a step back.

Christian shook his head. "Come with me, I'll explain."

FIVE

Christian picked up a big jug of water with a grunt. I crossed my arms and stared at him.

"Okay, seriously, what's going on here?" I asked.

"Oh, right," Christian said setting the jug back down. "So, first, let me start by saying I didn't realize Molly and Nick were like a thing."

I released a heavy sigh. "That's what this is about. She told us you made a pass at her."

"What?" Christian said with a laugh. "That's what she said? Oh, okay, I guess."

"Yeah, is that not what happened?" I asked.

"I'm not going to start any trouble," Christian said.

I shook my head. "Seems to me you've already started trouble."

"Look, she came on to me," Christian said holding up his hand. "It is what it is. She backed off almost instantly saying she was sorry and had made a mistake."

"This is what you and Nick bonded over?" I asked skeptically.

Christian snorted. "Not even a little. I think he plans to kill me."

"So, you invite him to stay at your house longer? And you want to leave with us?" I sighed. "None of this makes any sense."

"I don't know, babe, I just want to get the hell out of here," Christian said. "And I'm pretty sure you guys are my last chance before I OD or drink myself to death."

"OD?" I asked.

Christian looked down at his feet. "You don't want to know."

"You're right. I don't. I also don't think you should come with us," I said feeling the tension in my jaw. "It's been less than twenty-four hours with you and already there are problems."

"I didn't cause them," Christian said pulling his shoulders back. "If your friend would have been upfront with me, there wouldn't be any problems."

"Dammit," I said pressing my hands to my face.

"I really should go talk to her but I just don't get it. What changed Nick's mind about you?"

Christian looked away and wiped his nose with the back of his hand. "You don't want to know."

"No, I really do want to know," I said narrowing my eyes.

He shook his head. "You really don't."

"Does this have something to do with...," my words trailed off and I hesitated.

Nick had been smiling. It hadn't been that long ago he'd been pissed... ready to hit the wall. He hated Christian but suddenly they were best buds. But it wasn't any of those things that made me realize what was going on. It had been his eyes.

Those round pupils.

The glassiness.

"You're an idiot, you know that?" I said taking several steps away from him as if he were carrying a contagious disease. "He had a problem before all of this. You just opened a door for him again. A door that is nearly impossible for him to close."

"I didn't know," Christian said.

"You can't come with us," I said walking away. I wanted to run down the hall but I managed to hold myself together.

Christian stood there watching me with a stupid

smile on his face. He wasn't evil, he was stupid. He was high.

When I got back to the room we'd been staying in, Nick was lying on the sofa staring up at the ceiling. His eyelids were half-closed but he wasn't asleep.

I stood over him. Looking down into his blank eyes.

"Hey, sis," he said after several minutes. "What's up?"

I took several slow breaths before I raised my hand and slapped him across the face. His head flopped to the side but it didn't wipe the stupid, sloppy smile from his face.

"Whoa, Gwen!" Bronx said walking over to me. "What's going on?"

"Ask my idiotic brother," I said throwing my arm into the air as Bronx took another careful step in my direction.

I shook my head. I tried to swallow but the back of my throat was dry and scratchy as if I'd swallowed dust.

"Gwen?" Bronx said looking around the room as if he was searching for a missing puzzle piece that would explain everything.

"I'll... I... I need air," I said walking as quickly as I

could out of the room.

My feet only took me about ten steps before I heard Molly crying. The bathroom door was open a crack and I could see her sitting on the toilet lid, her shoulders bobbing as she sobbed.

I pushed open the door and closed it behind me. She looked up at me and then away as if she had hoped it would have been someone else. Nick? Christian?

I didn't know. I didn't care.

"He's high," I said trying to slow my rapid breathing. "I don't know what he said to you but he's so freaking high he probably has no idea what he said to you either."

"It doesn't matter," Molly said. "It's over."

"Christian said you came on to him. Why did you lie to us?"

Molly wiped a tear with the back of her hand. "It was a mistake. I was swept up in the moment. I stopped it nearly right away."

"You should have just told us the truth."

"I didn't think anyone would understand. Or care," Molly said. "He's going to leave me here you know that, right?"

"Nick?" I shook my head. "He's not going to leave you here. I won't let him do that to you."

Everything was just a mess. I didn't know what to do or say to fix any of it. If I even could.

"Maybe I should just stay here. He doesn't want me anywhere near him, he made that perfectly clear," Molly said, she looked at me with her red eyes. "I screwed things up so much. I don't even know where to start to fix them."

"I don't know," I said shaking my head. "You'll both have to find a way to work through this or at the very least a way to get along. We're not leaving you behind. Nick is a mess. I should have warned you about him."

Molly started sobbing again. "I really thought he was the one, Gwen. If things would have been different. We would have been getting married in Cabo or something."

And probably divorced less than a year later. Not that I was about to say that out loud.

"That Blair stuff screwed him up," Molly said. "Hell, it screwed me up."

"You guys will figure it out. Just give him some space." I bit my cheek before opening my mouth again. "And some time for him to come back down to earth."

It was weird but if Nick really would consider leaving Molly behind, I would have stayed with her.

Nick had the gun and the courage to venture forward but I wasn't going to let him leave people behind. There were enough assholes out there that we didn't need another.

"What you need to do is to get out of this bathroom and get something to eat. Some rest," I said placing my hands on her shoulders and helping her to her feet.

Molly looked at me as if I'd lost my mind. I exhaled slowly. "Sorry. Christian said I could take a bath. I really need a bath."

"There are probably twenty bathtubs in this building," Molly said with a frown.

"This one is the closest." I smiled and raised a brow. "Besides, can you tell me I'm wrong? I mean, you do need rest, we all do. And who doesn't want to fill up on all the yummies Christian has in the kitchen?"

"Fine," Molly said. "But don't say I never did anything for you."

I led her out of the bathroom. "Of course not. Never."

She started toward the room where Christian had serenaded her the first night. She didn't want to even be in the same room as Nick.

"Want to help me get the water?" I asked.

Molly groaned and turned on her heel. "Fine."

SIX

Molly and I set down the big jug of water in the hallway just in front of the bathroom door. She kicked it lightly with her foot.

"You're going to help me with one later, right?" she asked.

"Of course."

"You better," she said crossing her arms as she turned away.

The distraction had been good for her but it had only been temporary. Just like a switch had flipped, she was back to being upset about Nick.

I pushed open the bathroom door and turned around to drag the jug of water with me. My arms were shaking from the work my muscles had been doing. I couldn't wait to soak them even if the water wouldn't be warm.

For a second, I wondered if I should go back to the kitchen and boil some of the water. I shook my head. It would take too long and by the time I got enough warm water back here, it would be cold again.

I closed the door and just as I was about to lock it, a foot jammed itself between the door and the frame. It was a shoe I recognized.

"Yes?" I said opening the door slowly.

"Molly told me where you were," Bronx said with a tiny smirk he was trying to hide.

"Did she?"

His head bobbed up and down. "She did."

"Yeah, I was about to take a nice, refreshing, cool bath," I said.

Bronx placed his hand on the door and pushed it toward me. He slid inside and closed it quickly behind him.

Our bodies were so close I could feel his breath dance across my already blushing cheeks.

"Didn't you hear what I said?" My words were as soft as a feather. I could feel the pace of my breathing quicken.

"Oh, yeah, I heard what you said," Bronx whispered into my ear as he let his lips lightly brush against my neck. "That's why I locked the door. You'll need someone to wash your back for you."

"Bronx," I said although I wasn't sure why I said his name. My thoughts were lost, it was the only thing I could think to say.

His lips kissed across my cheek. My eyes closed when he found my mouth.

At first, his kiss was sweet... soft... gentle. But then his mouth pressed harder with a hunger that made my heart skip beats.

"They'll wonder where you are." I finally was able to get some words out.

"Let them wonder." Bronx's hands slid down the sides of my body stopping at the hem of my shirt. "It's not like they'll bust their way in here. Molly's busy sobbing, Christian is playing his guitar softly in the other room and Nick is... um, still resting."

"Resting," I repeated with a chuckle. My anger over what Nick had done completely disappeared as Bronx yanked my shirt over my head.

Bronx looked down at his feet. "He cried after you left."

"I don't care. If you think this is the first time he's

gotten high and faked regret, you'd be mistaken," I said squeezing my eyebrows together.

"It seemed like real regret," Bronx said.

"He's a good actor. That's probably why Molly is head over heels for him." I let out a heavy sigh, trying to rid my body of the tension that was building up.

Bronx looked up. His hands cupped my face and he looked into my eyes. "I don't want to talk about it anymore, do you?"

"No," I said letting my head fall back as his hands slide down the front of my body. "I definitely do not. All I want is to take my bath."

"Is that all you want?" Bronx said pulling my body tight against his. I could feel every inch of his need.

My knees weakened and my body felt like it was melting. I thought I was going to fall to the ground when Bronx abruptly let go.

He grabbed the jug of water, carrying it as if it weighed nothing.

"Where were you ten minutes ago?" I asked.

"All you had to do was ask and I would have been there," Bronx said pouring the water into the tub.

"I didn't even have to ask... you're still here," I

said softly as I stepped up behind him placing my hands on his back.

My hands moved down to the hem of his shirt and I pushed it up exposing his perfect, silky smooth skin. After he finished pouring the jug of water, he yanked off his shirt.

Our skin touching was akin to igniting a fire. Prickles of heat popped throughout every nerve-ending in my body and there wasn't a single thing I could do to stop the fire from raging through my body.

It felt like I was in a fog as my hands moved quickly to undo the button on Bronx's jeans. It was strange how time seemed to move both fast and slow at the same time.

Bronx's touch was like little firecrackers exploding on my skin. It was exhilarating.

My hands glided down his chest as his hands worked to remove the rest of my clothing. There wasn't an inch of fabric left on my body as he helped ease me into the tub.

"Brrr," I said but I'd barely noticed the temperature of the water.

Bronx climbed in the tub lowering himself down on top of me. The large tub didn't have much water but I barely noticed that either. All I could notice was the drop-dead gorgeous man on top of me. Kissing me. Touching me.

Every.

Single.

Inch.

Bronx was like a drug to me. When I was with him like this... I lost control. It was like I became someone else. And I really liked the person I became.

She was powerful.

She was in control.

She knew what she wanted.

And she didn't give a damn what anyone else thought. She deserved her happiness even if it was brief. I deserved that happiness.

In the world we currently lived in, everyone deserved something good. Bronx was my something good. If I wouldn't have had something, I wouldn't have anything to fight for.

Bronx grabbed the soap and slid it down my back. He worked up a lather and spread it across my chest.

"Mmm," I moaned as I leaned into him.

I took the bar of soap and ran it over his rock-hard chest. He didn't give me a chance to work up many bubbles before his weight was on top of me.

Bronx groaned as he worked his way inside me. I bit my lip and wrapped my legs around him.

The water splashed around us as we slipped around inside the tub as one. Bronx's arm wrapped around my hips, holding me tightly to him.

"Gwen," he whispered before he hungrily placed his mouth on mine. His lips moved with the pace of his hips. It was achingly slow and I wanted nothing more than to have my release.

It was as if he knew how badly I wanted to let go but he was making me wait until I couldn't take it any longer. Increasing my need. Increasing my desire.

"Bronx, please," I said sounding as if I was begging.

He flashed me an intoxicated grin. "Baby not yet... not yet...."

"Bronx...," I moaned.

"Who knows when we'll get a chance like this again," Bronx said his voice low. "We need to enjoy it."

I sucked in a quick breath. "I am enjoying it."

Bronx stopped moving and starting lightly dragging his fingertips down my cheek... my chin... my neck... my breast.

I shivered. I couldn't take it. My release was

going to find its way out and there wasn't going to be anything I could do to stop it.

All it took was his touch. Just being with him like this was enough to launch me off of the cliff of my pleasure.

Bronx started to move again, slowly. His hand on my lower back, holding me so tightly against him.

My breathing was short and then slow and then back to short again. I was losing myself and it was amazing.

Bronx's thumb lightly touched my chin and he angled my head slightly so my gaze met his. He moved quicker. "Okay, baby. Okay."

"Ooh," I said as my body tensed. It felt like my body was rising up to the sky, as if I was on a roller coaster ride and we were climbing to the top of a hill.

My fingertips dug into Bronx's back as we reached the top of the ride. I held on as if my life depended on it, as we crashed back down to the ground together.

Every muscle in my body relaxed at the same moment. It felt like I was in an ocean of bliss and I was floating on the surface.

"Oh, God," I said jolting upward. The coldness of the water hit me like a baseball bat to the head. It felt like I was lying on a bed of ice cubes.

I climbed out of the tub and grabbed the nearest towel. Shivers rippled up and down my body.

Bronx was behind me in an instant rubbing his hands on my arms. "You're freezing."

"Yeah, I guess I am," I said turning into his chest.

"Let's get you dressed," he said picking up my clothes off the floor and handing them to me. "I'll get a fire going in the other room. Need to warm you up."

"I just need to be in your arms," I said placing a kiss on his cheek.

Bronx tightened his arms. "I wish I never had to let go."

"Who said you do?" I asked.

"We can't stay in this bathroom forever," Bronx said giving me a squeeze before turning me toward the mirror and pointing at the clothes bunched up in my arm. "You'll freeze to death."

"No, yeah, I know," I said with a half-frown. "It's just that—"

"Yeah, this is what I'm living for too," Bronx said. "One day things will be different."

I snorted and pulled on my shirt. "No, it won't. This is our life now."

"Your glass is always half-empty," Bronx said pulling on his pants.

"I'm being realistic," I said with a shrug.

Bronx shook his head and smiled. "I'll be positive for the both of us. But the truth is, I don't care where I am as long as I'm with you."

His words made my heart melt. And suddenly, just like that, my body was warm again.

SEVEN

In the morning, Nick was up and ready to go. He and Christian had packed a couple extra bags of supplies while the rest of us had slept.

Nick's eyes were red and I wondered if he had gotten any sleep at all. For all I knew, he'd taken another hit of whatever Christian had given him to keep himself going.

Everyone was clean and in new clothes. Each one of us wearing a t-shirt with Christian's band logo on it. It looked like we were all in some kind of strange uniform.

Christian and Nick had seemingly become best friends. It made me almost positive that Christian had packed more of whatever he'd given Nick.

Molly followed along dragging her feet behind

us. Her eyes were red and swollen from all the tears she'd shed over my jerk of a brother. I guess, technically, this time she'd been the jerk but I was used to Nick being at fault.

I wanted to talk some sense into Nick, tell him what Molly had told me. She'd been swept up in the moment.

Christian was a bit on the thin side but he was good looking. He was the type of guy I would have thought Molly would be with, not my brother. Maybe for a brief moment, she thought that too.

If it were meant to be, it would work out. I wasn't going to get involved like I had tried to with Blair. Nick would have to make his own mistakes and live with the consequences. Just like he'd have to live with what Blair had done to herself.

All my life, I'd tried to fix things for Nick but I was done. Not once had he listened to me. I was done wasting my time.

There was a strange noise that cut through my thoughts like a blade. I scrunched up my nose at the odd hoof-hoof-hoof noise that cut through the crisp morning air.

"What is that?" I asked glancing at Bronx. He shook his head. "You hear that, right?"

"I do but I have no idea what that could be,"

Bronx said his eyes darting around. He lowered his voice. "Another attack? We should find shelter."

"It's not an attack," Nick said tilting his head toward the sky. "It's a helicopter."

My breath felt like it was stuck inside my nostrils. "They weren't lying."

"Who wasn't lying?" Christian asked.

"Some people we met," Nick said. "Said they saw helicopters."

"They also said there was a safe place to go in Canada," Bronx added.

Christian stared up at the sky. "You didn't believe them?"

"It's hard to know what to believe," Nick said with a shrug. "It's a dog-eat-dog world out here. People building armies. People are desperate and when they're desperate, they'll do terrible things."

"But there is a helicopter up in the sky," Christian said. "I'd love to be rescued."

"They said help is in Winnipeg. You're free to go," Nick said his words icy. "But it's a risk I'm not willing to take."

"You're just going to find your own place and hide out for the rest of your lives?" Christian asked. "Don't you want to find civilization again?"

Nick turned to him and didn't blink. "It doesn't exist. It's a trick."

"You don't know that," I said sharply.

Nick turned and glared at me. "You're free to go too."

"I know I am," I said feeling the tension building in my jaw. "And trust me, if I ever want to leave, I will. You don't have to worry about that. For now, I don't think there is anything out there for me."

Christian stared at me for a moment. He was considering everything that had been said.

In the silence, I listened for the noises again but they weren't there. If the others wouldn't have heard it as well, I would have thought I had imagined it.

"It stopped," Molly said softly. "Maybe it wasn't a helicopter at all."

Nick looked up at the sky as he spun in a slow circle. There wasn't anything in sight except for the thick heavy clouds hanging in the sky threatening to hide the sun.

"Let's keep going," Nick said. "Even if it was a helicopter, they weren't here for us. Who knows who they were or what they'd do to us."

Bronx and I exchanged a glance. There was a small part of me that wondered if maybe the whole Winnipeg thing was true. Maybe there was a sanctuary but did that mean it was somewhere that was safe? It could have just been another base where someone like Tom was in charge. And that was not somewhere I wanted to be. Traveling to Winnipeg was a risk. A risk we were not willing to take.

We kept walking mostly in silence. I wondered if Nick was thinking about the helicopter because I couldn't stop thinking about it. Maybe that was why I wasn't talking... I was waiting to see if I'd hear the noises again but I didn't. We were surrounded by an eerie, uncomfortable silence that no one was willing to break. At least, not until we came upon what appeared to be an abandoned trailer park.

It was midday and we didn't need to find a place to stop for the night but a break was needed. Plus, it was always worth checking out random buildings for supplies or food. If they had food and water, we wouldn't need to use our own.

"We'll start with this one," Nick said pointing at the first tan and yellow trailer with huge rust spots on the sides. "Two inside the rest keep watch."

"Who's going in?" Bronx asked.

"Me... and Molly," Nick said without looking at her.

Molly looked at me for a long moment her eyes

were wide with confusion. She looked happy and worried at the same time.

Bronx leaned back against the side of the trailer near the door. He kept his hands at his sides as his eyes moved around the trailer park.

Christian paced around in the small driveway where a car normally would have been parked. I hoped that it was a good sign that the car was gone. That would mean that whoever had lived here had been gone when the sky turned red. Of course, that didn't mean they hadn't come back or that someone else had moved in, but since I hadn't heard any gunshots, I had to hope there wasn't anyone home.

I could hear Nick and Molly moving around inside of the trailer. The thin walls didn't hide their movements as they walked over the squeaky floor.

The sounds softened as they made their way to the far end of the trailer. Then, the sounds stopped.

Several minutes ticked by before Christian started cracking his knuckles nervously. He drew in a sharp breath that pulled in his stomach.

"What's taking them so long?" Christian asked. "Is this what it's like?"

"What it's like?" I asked.

"Being out here? Is it always so nerve-wracking?" Christian said.

I chuckled. "This is nerve-wracking? This is nothing."

"What are they doing in there? It's like the size of my bathroom," Christian said.

"They're being thorough," I said but they were taking a longer than I would have liked. I assumed they were talking because I couldn't hear the squeaks and creaks any longer.

It was at least another five minutes before the noises of them moving about started up again. They emerged, Nick came out first and Molly was behind him with her head down.

"Next," Nick said gesturing at the faded blue trailer less than ten steps away. "Bronx, show Christian what we do."

"Sure," Bronx said jiggling the locked door as he peered inside. He turned to Nick and shook his head.

"Break it down," Nick said scrunching up his nose as he drew in a quick sniff.

Bronx looked at me over his shoulder and then back at Nick. "Sure, about that? Might make too much noise."

"I'm sure," Nick said. "Need me to do it?"

The door was so flimsy I was pretty sure that I could break it down with a kick near the doorknob.

"I got it, bro," Bronx said less than a second before throwing his shoulder into the door. The whole door dented inward with a loud crack as it popped back and hit the wall inside. "Piece of cake."

Before they could step inside something in rustled in the bushes behind me. I turned on my heel and took a step back.

All I could see was the end of a barrel pointed directly at me. I couldn't move my eyes but I could feel others popping out from our surroundings.

"Bob," the one with the gun pointed at me shouted. "Bob, they broke your door."

A heavy man came out from behind one of the trailers and pushed past the guy holding the gun at me. He bumped into him so hard the guy lost his balance and had to aim up his gun again.

Bob stomped closer and adjusted the camouflage baseball cap on his head. He pointed his thick finger at Bronx. "You're going to pay for that!"

EIGHT

Nick stepped over and blocked the large man's path. Bob wasn't just twice Nick's width, he was also several inches taller.

Bob touched the wiry, gray whiskers on his chin as he looked down at Nick. His hand shot forward and he wrapped his fingers around Nick's neck.

"Whoa," Nick choked out the word as his hands waved at his sides.

Bronx pushed me behind him and he went toward the man. He didn't care how many guns were pointed at them.

"Hold on there," another man said. "Unless you want me to put a bullet in the back of her pretty little head."

"Holy shit," Christian said taking a step back. He would have kept going but the trailer stopped him.

Bronx stopped and held up his hands. "We didn't know anyone was here. I apologize for breaking your door. We were just looking for supplies."

"Looks to me like you have enough supplies," Bob said his eyes jerking toward the bag Christian was holding.

"You can never have enough," Bronx said. "Please," he said slowly gesturing to Nick, "let him breathe."

Bob looked at Nick and then laughed. Nick's face was so red it looked like his head was going to pop right off of his neck.

"Sorry about that," he said loosening his grip slightly. He shook his head. "Oh, wait, no, I'm not. You little pieces of shit come here and break my property. I don't feel even a little sorry."

"We're so sorry," Bronx said.

"Sorry ain't gonna fix my door!" Bob spat. After a moment, he released a deep breath and threw Nick down to the ground. "You guys need to pay for that. It's going to take me at least a day to find a new door and replace it."

Nick placed his hands on his neck as if making

sure it was still there. He didn't bother to get up. "A whole day, huh?"

Bob moved quickly as he stepped forward and kicked Nick in the thigh. Nick winced and swallowed down a howl as he hands moved up and down his leg... the leg that hadn't fully healed from when he'd been shot.

"You're a little smart ass, aren't you? You want to find out what we do to smart asses?" Bob asked and his minions laughed and hooted.

"I want to see it, boss," the tall one holding Molly said.

Tears were streaming down Molly's face. She was so still she looked as though she'd turned into a statue. A terrified statue.

"We're terribly sorry for breaking your door," Bronx said holding up his hands. "If we knew anyone was here, it wouldn't have happened. What can we do to make it up to you?"

"We'll take her," the tall man holding Molly said.

Nick's ears turned red with anger. He looked like he was going to throw himself at the tall man but if he did, that would only get him killed. And maybe Molly too. It didn't seem as if Nick realized that.

"We can't let you do that," Bronx said. "Anything else, hell, if you want me to fix it, I'm pretty handy."

Bob laughed. "The last thing we want is you idiots hanging around here snooping through our things."

"Fair enough," Bronx said. "So, if you let her go, we'll get out of your hair."

"Well we need some kind of payment," Bob said scratching his beard.

Bronx's shoulders rose up and pushed back as he let out a deep exhale. We all waited in silence for Bob's price.

"Your bags," Bob said squeezing his eyebrows together as if he wasn't sure that was enough. But, then, his head bobbed up and down more enthusiastically. "Yeah, your bags."

"You can't take all our stuff," Nick said.

"We'll let you keep one," Bob said. "Of course, then we get to keep her. Choice is yours."

We handed over our things but I was afraid that they wouldn't follow through. I had to hope that Nick had a backup plan that involved his gun.

"That one too," Bob said gesturing at Nick's pack.

Nick picked up his bag and whipped it toward the guy holding Molly. It lightly hit him in the legs.

The tall man laughed but then the smile instantly fell off his face. He let go of Molly.

"Go on," the man said. The second she took a step, he pushed her hard, throwing her back in much the same way Nick had thrown the bag.

Molly stumbled forward with her hands out in front of her. Nick tried to stretch out his arms to catch her but she fell several feet short of where he was. Her cheek hit the ground and when she looked up at him, I could see drops of blood oozing out of the small scrapes on her skin.

Nick kept his arms out and Molly scurried toward him as fast as a cockroach hiding from the light. He wrapped his arms around her and looked up at the tall man. I could see nothing but hate in his eyes. It surprised me that Nick hadn't pulled out his gun and killed the man in exchange from his own life.

"Now, if you would all be so kind as to get the hell out of our territory," Bob said placing his thick sausage hands on his hips.

Bronx stood between me and as many of the trailer park people as he could. Christian looked like he was going to be sick but eventually got his feet moving.

I could hear them laughing as we practically ran from the area and it was clear that the noises coming from behind us were agitating Nick. The tendons in his neck popped out.

"I should go back there," Nick growled as he pulled out his gun. "Get out stuff back. They won't be expecting it."

Bronx was shaking his head. He didn't manage to get a single word out before Nick turned on his heel and started to go back there.

"Wait here," Nick said.

"Whoa," Bronx said taking large steps to catch up to him. "That's a terrible idea. We'll get more stuff."

"I should go back home," Christian said looking off in the distance.

Nick faced Christian. "No one is keeping you here."

Christian took a step back as if Nick had punched him in the face.

"Everyone needs to calm down," Bronx said. He looked into Nick's rage-filled eyes. "No one is going back there. We will find more stuff." Bronx turned to Christian. "If you think that was bad, maybe you should go back home, the only problem is, no one is going to take you back home. What would you do if someone like they came into your home? You're not prepared."

"I could hide," Christian mumbled.

"Yeah, you could. Or you can just come with us and hide. At least one way you aren't alone," Bronx said throwing his hands in the air. "But the choice is yours."

Nick pushed his shoulders back. "But the choice to go back there isn't mine?"

"Your head isn't on straight right now," Bronx said. "You're just looking for revenge. That's just going to get you killed."

"I want our stuff back," Nick said his eyes bulging out of their sockets.

"One verses like ten isn't smart, Nick, you know that," Bronx said shaking his head. "Don't worry about the stuff. Molly's safe. You're safe. We're all safe. Let's just keep moving."

Nick grabbed my arm. He stared into my eyes for a moment.

"You've been awfully quiet," Nick said almost sneering at me. "If you think I should go back there, speak up. Don't hold it in because you disagree with him."

I snorted. "I don't disagree with him. You should not go back there."

Nick threw his hands in the air and shook his head. He ran his shaking fingers through his hair.

"If we die because we run out of supplies, then what?" Nick asked.

"We'll find more," Bronx said confidently.

"I give up," Nick said. There were beads of sweat sprinkled along his forehead and temples. I wondered if he was dealing with some kind of withdrawal.

He was aggressive.

He was sweaty.

And he wasn't quite himself. But the last thing I wanted to do was to bring it up. It would only make him angrier.

"Let's get moving," Bronx said.

Nick opened his mouth to say something but closed it. He pressed his palms to his face and his shoulders dropped with his exhale.

He looked at me and then at Molly. The blood on her face from where she'd been scratched was smeared toward her nose. Her eyes were swollen and filled with fear.

Nick blinked twice. "Argh! Okay. Let's go."

NINE

Nick didn't say another word for several hours. He held Molly's hand as we walked at a quick pace.

I wasn't sure if whatever they had talked about inside the trailer before we were ambushed had something to do with it or if Molly being held captive had made Nick come to his senses. It was interesting that he seemed to be fighting for Molly. In fact, the main reason he had probably wanted to go back to the trailer park was to get back at them for having held her against her will.

One thing that was frustrating about running into people was that now we were going to have to travel further before we could find our secluded hideaway. We'd put in so many miles already, and now we'd have to put in many, many more.

I looked up at the sky that seemed to be getting darker quicker than normal. Every day was colder than the last but the walking had always been enough to keep me warm. The nights had been hard but the blankets we had in our packs had helped when we weren't able to have a fire. Now, we had nothing.

"Look at those clouds," Bronx said pointing at the darkness in the distance.

"Yeah... what about them?" I asked squinting at the black fluffs hanging low in the sky.

"Do they look unusual to you?" he asked.

I shrugged. "They're dark. Maybe a storm?"

"Yeah, maybe," Bronx said each word slowly. "I don't like storms."

"I don't either," I said.

Bronx looked glanced over his shoulder. "We're going to need to find a place to stop for the night."

"I've been looking," Nick said from behind.

Christian stepped up beside me. "This is what it's like? Every day?"

"I guess we should have been more clear about all this," I said.

"Nick was clear," Christian said. "I guess it was just hard to believe it could really be this bad."

"Sorry," I said. It was all I could manage to say.

Christian hadn't been outside of his mansion since the red sky had come. It wasn't surprising that it was going to be a shock. And maybe we'd find out that it was a mistake to leave his place behind but he'd probably been lucky that no one had come around. Christian was lucky that the first people to come upon his property were us.

We continued for at least an hour before finding a small broken-down barn and a small home where the roof had caved in.

"This is going to have to do," Nick said spinning around with his hands on his hips.

The dark, heavy clouds hadn't moved but they gave the sky a new darkness that would make traveling at night even more difficult. We were lucky we didn't have to try to navigate the night.

"Molly and I will check the house for supplies," Nick said jerking his head toward what was left of the building. "You guys check out the barn."

"I'm not sure you should go in there," I said biting my lip.

"Afraid it's haunted?" Nick said with a little

smile. It was the first time I'd seen a brightness to his expression in days.

I chuckled and shook my head as I crossed my arms. "Well, it looks like it might be but more importantly it looks like it's going to crumble to the ground at any moment."

"Then you won't have to worry about me anymore," Nick said letting the smile fall from his face.

My stomach twisted into a tight knot. That wasn't at all what I wanted but I didn't know how to tell him that because I was still frustrated, no, I was still angry with him.

"It's not going to fall on top of us. If I was at all worried about that, there is no way I would bring Molly with me," Nick said wrapping his arm around her shoulder.

She looked at him with love in her eyes but there was also a sadness there I didn't understand. I wondered if it was because of the mistake she'd made with Christian or if it had been there because of something else. Maybe I wouldn't ever know and maybe I didn't need to know.

After countless times of trying to fix Nick and help him correct mistakes, I'd never been able to help him. What I needed was to let go. The only problem was that it was impossible for me to be there for him after he made his mistakes.

At Christian's mansion, he'd fallen again and it only made me angrier with him. It was impossible to be okay with that but perhaps my relationship with Nick wouldn't ever be what I had wanted it to be.

I still had my brother but the truth was, I'd lost him years ago. I'd mourned that loss and I didn't want to ever mourn him again.

We would just have to work together for survival, no different from what I would do with Molly, Christian, and Bronx. There was no point in wishing he was someone he wasn't ever going to be.

It seemed as though everyone that we ran into that found out he was my brother always said how lucky we were to have each other. In our case, I wasn't sure it was true.

Christian and I followed Bronx into the barn. My feet squished into the damp soil

I shivered as I looked around the emptied barn. There wasn't anything inside, not even a single rusted tool. It made me worried that someone was close by but I had to hope that whoever had cleaned out the barn was long gone.

"It's so cold," Christian said. "Can we start a fire?"

"Hmm," Bronx said tapping his chin. "I don't think so."

I was shaking my head before Bronx finished speaking. "It would draw too much attention out in the open like this."

"The smoke from my chimney could have drawn attention but you didn't care about that," Christian said.

"There were a lot of trees blocking the area," Bronx said. "The flames were hidden inside the fireplace and the night sky hid the smoke."

Christian frowned. "We're going to freeze to death out here."

"It's cold but it's not that cold," Bronx said drawing in a deep breath. "Maybe Nick and Molly have found some blankets."

"We didn't find shit," Nick said busting into the barn empty-handed. "Everything has been destroyed or cleaned out."

"So, we're going to freeze to death," Christian said.

Nick chuckled. "We're not going to freeze to death. Dehydration is going to get us before that happens."

"Nick!" Molly said slapping him in the bicep.

"What?" Nick asked with a laugh. He held up

his hand. "Okay, okay, sorry! We're not going to die. At least not tonight... not from hypothermia and not from dehydration."

Bronx shook his head as he carried some of the dry hay into the corner of the room. He started to pat it down on top of the dirt.

"We'll huddle up in there," Bronx said pointing over his shoulder as he walked over to grab more hay.

"And what about food?" Christian asked.

"We'll find something tomorrow," I said before Nick could say something negative or make a joke that Christian surely wouldn't find amusing.

We huddled up in the room on top of the hay. Molly and Nick sat next to me and Bronx, and Christian sat down across from us with his back against the wall. He had his arms wrapped around himself.

"You'll be warmer if you come closer," I said pointing at the space next to Bronx.

Christian held up his hand. "I'm fine."

"Don't be stubborn," Nick said.

"I said I was fine," Christian said lowering his head. His unblinking eyes focused on his shoes. I could tell he was regretting having left his mansion and I wasn't sure I blamed him.

"Things will get better than this," I said flashing Christian a thin-lipped smile.

He nodded but still kept his eyes down. Even though he was with us, I could tell he was feeling very alone.

"I need a moment," Christian said standing up. He took three steps toward the doorway before turning to face Nick. "Want to join me?"

"No, thank you," Nick said swallowing hard. I met his eyes for a split second and instantly realized what he was turning down.

"Okay," Christian said wiping his nose. "I'll be right back."

I smiled at Nick but he had already turned back to Molly. She relaxed her shoulders as she rested her head down on Nick's arm.

When Christian returned, he looked much calmer. He also looked as if he wasn't exactly sure where he was.

Christian sat down and rested his head back against the wall. He looked up at the cracked ceiling with a stupid smile on his face. Christian no longer looked cold, but there was no way we could trust him to take a turn keeping watch which wasn't a big deal considering Nick probably wouldn't have allowed it anyway.

I sighed and pulled my legs closer to my body. It was going to be hard to get any sleep and not because of the cold or the damp ground.

"I'll take the first watch," I offered knowing it was going to take more for me to be able to close my eyes. The truth was, I didn't think I'd sleep and I couldn't wait until morning.

"You sure?" Bronx asked with a yawn.

"Positive," I said and he kissed me on the top of the head.

I sat there in silence letting the minutes tick by. My body was sore and tired but my mind was restless.

I couldn't stop thinking about what Christian was hiding in his pockets and wondering if Nick would be able to continue to decline his offer. Eventually, whatever he had with him would run out. Then we'd have to deal with Christian going through withdrawal.

I'd seen Nick go through withdrawal multiple times. He was family and I couldn't stand to deal with it. There was no way I would be able to be there for a stranger. It was bad enough to sit there and let him do that to himself.

I sighed and pressed my palm to my forehead.

We needed to find our place soon because until we did, sleep was going to be hard.

My head tipped back with my quick yawn and as I closed my mouth, an unusual noise filled the air. It sounded like someone was bending a large sheet of metal.

The creaking and grinding noise was like finger-nails on a chalkboard but it was so far away that it didn't wake the others. At first, I wasn't sure if I had heard it at all, but when it happened again, I knew for sure that I had.

I tapped Bronx on the shoulder. "Bronx," I whispered. "Wake up!"

TEN

"What is that?" Bronx asked as Nick stood up to peer out of the cracked window.

I could barely see Molly picking at her fingers in the darkness. The whites of her wide eyes were practically lighting the room.

"It sounds like a plane falling from the sky," Molly said in a low scratchy voice. She frowned and her eyes closed slightly as she slouched down as if she were trying to hide.

Nick nodded. "But there are no planes."

"There are no planes around here, but maybe there are planes elsewhere. Just because everything stopped working around us doesn't mean they stopped working everywhere," I said trying to sound confident about what I was saying.

"No, it's not a plane," Nick said as if he knew for a fact.

"Then what do you think it is, smart ass?" I asked.

He shook his head. "I don't know. Another attack?"

"Oh, God," I said looking up at the roof. "Not here... we're not safe."

"Why didn't I just stay home?" Christian moaned through his stupor. He wouldn't know what was happening until it was done.

"Relax," Nick said. "If it's another attack, it's not happening right here."

I shook my head in frustration. "They can move. We've seen them move. Remember the blue cloud?"

"Of course I remember, but it's not moving now," Nick said. "It's probably just a storm in the distance and we're over-reacting."

"Whatever it is, I'm not going to be able to sleep now," Molly said with a yawn. "That was terrifying."

Nick's eyebrows squeezed together. "If it weren't so dark out there, I'd say we should just put in some miles but without any light from the moon, it's too hard to see. I can barely see a foot in front of me."

I sat there staring at the wall waiting for the noise to happen again. If I could hear it, maybe I could figure out what it was that was making the noise. But it didn't happen again.

Nick continued to pace the rest of the night. And I sat there watching him. The only one that had been able to get any rest was Christian but then again, I wasn't sure if passing out could be called sleep.

When the first bit of morning light came, we headed out of the barn. My eyes darted around in every direction but nothing seemed out of the ordinary. Of course, that didn't mean I was about to stop worrying.

The dark clouds were still hanging in the sky in the far distance. It didn't seem as though they had moved at all.

The air was still quite chilly but walking helped to keep me warm. It wasn't until midday when we saw a small town in the distance and my grumbling stomach hoped we'd find something to eat.

"So, do we go into the town or do we keep on going?" Christian asked. His eyelids drooped down hooding half of his crystal blue eyes.

"We go in," Nick said with his chin pointed forward. "We're armed. What's there to be afraid of?"

I shook my head at his massive amount of over-confidence. "They were also armed at the trailer park. Our guns didn't help much back there, did they? There is a ton to be afraid of."

"It's not all bad," Nick said smiling at Molly. "Not everyone out there is bad."

"No, of course not," I said rolling my eyes. "But, as you know, there are people that are. And it's not just people that we have to worry about. Animals. Weird attacks. Hell, eating the wrong thing."

My eyes darted over to the thick, darkish purple clouds still hanging in the air. I was worried about them. My stomach swirled as if it were filled with twenty tornadoes just looking at the clouds. I was probably more worried about the strange weather than I was about the potentially bad people waiting for us in the small town.

The stop in town had been easy. If anyone had been hiding, they kept themselves that way. Maybe there were people that were just as afraid of us as we would be of them.

We spent the next several days traveling without seeing another soul. There was food and water along the way but not enough that we could pack it up and take it with us. It was going to take us weeks to build up enough supplies to get back to what we had before it had been taken from us at the trailer park.

I wasn't sure how long we'd been traveling but it

had probably been at least a week since we'd left the barn. Nick had been trying to find our perfect hideout but he wasn't satisfied with anything and I was almost certain he wouldn't ever be. He wouldn't ever find anywhere that he would feel safe.

The night was setting in earlier and earlier and along with it came the cold. We'd found jackets which helped to keep us warm but it wasn't as nice as starting a fire would have been. My bones felt as though they were made of icicles.

"Let's check out those houses," Nick said gesturing at a small cluster of country homes.

"What's the use? Everything's been taken," Christian groaned. Each mile we traveled he was more and more pessimistic... more grumpy. More difficult to be around.

I was pretty sure that his secret stash had been dwindling, which hopefully, meant that when he actually ran out of whatever it was, withdrawal would be slightly easier because of the weaning off of it over time. But then again, maybe it wouldn't be.

We didn't even make it to the first house before we heard sobbing. I couldn't see the woman it was coming from but it was clear she wasn't making any effort to keep her cries quiet.

"Oh dear, where could he be?" she asked before

slamming something shut. A cupboard door? "It's gone," she continued between deep sniffs. "It's all gone."

We stood there staring at the back of the building. There was nowhere to hide in the wide-open area except for a broken-down fence that had once completely surrounded the property. There were so many missing pieces, cracks, and holes that it didn't do a good job of hiding us at all.

"Should we run?" Molly asked.

Nick placed his hand on her shoulder and guided her lower to the ground. His voice was feather soft. "No."

A woman stepped out of the back door wiping her already reddened, raw cheeks. She froze instantly and blinked several times. There was no doubt in my mind that she was looking right at us.

ELEVEN

The woman cocked her head to the side and hesitated for a long moment before flipping it to the other side. Her eyes narrowed as she stared forward.

"Hello?" she called sounding like she was asking us a question. She placed her hands on her hips. The woman wasn't holding a weapon but she did have a shotgun slung over her shoulder. "I can see you all. Why are you attempting to hide from me?"

"Are you alone?" Nick called out without standing.

The woman's eyes focused right on the spot where Nick was crouched down. She crossed her arms and didn't even try to hide the fact that she was annoyed by us.

"Yeah, I'm all alone," she said as her shoulders slumped down. "I'm looking for someone... maybe you can help me?"

Nick drew in a breath and glanced over at me before standing. His gun was in his hand and if the woman noticed, she didn't seem to care.

The woman took a step closer, hobbling ever so slightly. She continued forward and as she drew nearer, I could see that she was a bit older than I had originally thought.

Her cheeks drooped slightly, and there were deep wrinkles at the corners of her eyes. When she smiled at us, the lines of her face softened.

"I'm Carol Ann," she said stretching out her hand. "And you are?"

"I'm Nick," he said as he took her hand into his. His face was scrunched up as if he didn't understand her politeness. It looked like he was expecting people to jump out from behind her and start attacking us.

"Good to meet you, Nick. And who are all your friends?" Carol Ann asked.

He pointed at us as he told her our names. "Christian, Molly, Bronx, and she's my sister, Gwen."

"Hello," Carol Ann said bobbing her head along with each name. "How nice to have family. I doubt mine have survived." The woman frowned for a moment before she shook her head and clicked her tongue. "Never mind that. I'll do my best to remember all your names but you may have to remind me... several times."

"No problem," Nick said, pointing at the building behind her with his chin. "Is this your home?"

Carol Ann shook her head. "It is not. I'm about five miles north of here."

"You probably shouldn't give strangers that information, ma'am," Nick said.

Carol Ann flapped her hand. "Oh, nonsense."

"What are you doing here?" Nick asked. Bronx and I moved closer to stand next to Nick and the woman smiled at us.

"I'm looking for my husband." Carol Ann frowned. Her eyes shifted upward and suddenly they filled with brightness. "Maybe you've seen him?"

Bronx shook his head. "We haven't seen anyone in quite a while."

The woman reached into the inside pocket of her jacket and pulled something out. She stared at the piece of paper for a moment before holding it out to Nick.

"This is him. Does he look familiar?" Carol Ann asked.

Nick took what I assumed was a photo and looked at it for a solid minute before handing it to Bronx.

"Sorry, I haven't," Nick said and Bronx shook his head before passing me the picture. I wished I could have told the woman I'd seen him but I was positive I hadn't.

"Shame," she said shaking her head. "He went out to check the town for more supplies as he often does. He hasn't come back yet. I'm really starting to get worried. Dick hasn't ever been gone this long."

"How long has it been?" I asked the woman.

She released a long sigh and scrunched up her nose. "I think it's been about a month. I haven't been very good at keeping track of time, although I do try."

"I can relate," I said giving her a tight-lipped smile. Except I had given up on even trying to keep track some time ago.

Carol Ann held my gaze for a moment as if she was trying to determine if I was serious or not. After a bit, she gave me a nod and tucked the picture back into her pocket.

"Say, you all look pretty weary from your travels. Would you like to come up to the house for some food and rest?" Carol Ann asked. "It'll be a bit of a hike but I have tons of food, water, and some nice cozy beds. All with brand new bedding."

"Why would you want to share?" Molly asked keeping herself half-behind Nick. "No one wants to share these days."

"Oh, nonsense! You haven't been meeting the right people," Carol Ann said crossing her arms as she shook her head. "My husband, Dick, and I have far more than we will ever be able to use on our own. Please, he'll be so thrilled to come home to guests. He'd been getting a little bored with just me around and I'm not sure I can blame him."

Carol Ann grinned so widely her eyes squeezed shut. It was too bad she couldn't find her husband because it was clear she loved him dearly. Her whole face lit up when she spoke of him even though I could see the worry in her eyes.

"Please," she said looking up to the sky. "It looks like a storm might roll in soon. You'll be glad to have a shelter when it does. And I'd love the company."

"Can you give us a minute to discuss it?" Nick asked.

"Oh, of course! Take all the time you need. I'll be next door if you need me," Carol Ann said before taking a backward step toward the neighboring house.

She turned and shoved her hands into her pockets. The woman didn't even look back at us over her shoulder. Carol Ann was unbelievably trusting and that made me worried about the woman. How had she survived this long?

"Think we should go with her?" Nick asked after she disappeared inside the building.

"It could be a trap," Bronx said but he dismissively shook his head. "But I don't think it is."

"Poor woman must be lost without her husband," Molly said rubbing her fingers together. "I can't even imagine what she must be going through."

Nick looked at the distant clouds. "She's right that a storm could be rolling in."

"How long can it be rolling in for?" I asked. "It doesn't seem to be moving."

"But when it does, it might be better to be someplace safe. Someplace that has food and water." Nick shook his head. "There's a chance that we might not find something else that has those things before the clouds reach us."

"If they reach us," I said.

Nick cocked his head to the side. "So, you don't think we should go with her?"

"I don't know what I think," I said crossing my arms. I turned to stare at the building she was inside of as if the answer should flash at me like a neon sign.

"I think it'll be fine. She's alone," Nick said.

"She's alone now but if she's leading us into a trap, it could be a town filled with people that were to skin us alive and devour our flesh for dinner," I said with a shiver.

Nick chuckled. "That's quite an imagination you have, Sis."

"People are desperate," I said chewing the already raw inside of my cheek. "They do desperate things."

"I don't think it's very likely that this woman wandering around looking for her husband is secretly trying to find people which she'll bring back to her cult so that they can eat them," Nick said.

"No, probably not likely," I said. "But is it impossible?"

Nick was smiling but it seemed to waver ever so slightly as he considered the question. "Well, we can decline her offer. Either way, I think she made a good point about finding shelter."

I stared at the clouds. Had they gotten closer? Why did they just hang there in the sky the way they did? Maybe it really was another attack, and it was inching closer and closer before it would explode and take out everything in its path. For all we knew, we wouldn't even make it to Carol Ann's home.

"Should we take a vote?" Nick asked.

I scratched the side of my head. It seemed silly to me that we would need to vote instead of just coming to an agreement.

"I vote we go to her house," Molly said with a slight shiver. "It's cold, I'm tired, and I'm scared. I want a break."

"We just had a break at Christian's," I said.

Molly frowned. "That was forever ago. I need another break."

"We'll have a permanent break when we find our place," I said with a half-shrug. "Then we'll probably have too much of a break and everyone will be complaining that they are bored."

"It sounds to me like you don't want to go," Nick said.

I threw my hands into the air. "Argh! I don't know what I want. It's not like it's completely up to me."

"I vote we check it out," Christian said softly. He didn't seem sure if his vote mattered. "I'm not used to all this walking."

I glanced at Bronx just as the woman stepped out

of the back door. She stopped and watched us for a moment before walking over to us.

Her smile looked like it had been drawn on her face with a red marker. "So, what's it going to be folks?"

"What do you think, Gwen?" Nick asked putting me on the spot.

I could feel the heat rising to my cheeks. I wanted to throw my fist into his jaw for putting all the weight on my shoulders.

My eyes landed on Bronx's and I tried to read his thoughts through them. If he felt strongly one way or the other, I couldn't figure out which was it was that he leaned.

"I'm not sure," I said.

"Oh gosh, it'll be absolutely fine, my dear!" Carol Ann said hooking her arm through mine. She started to lead me away from the group. "I have yarn and books, even an old typewriter. You won't be bored and you won't be hungry." She patted my hand and leaned closer. "You could handle putting on a few pounds."

I wasn't sure if anyone had ever told me that in my entire life. My fingers did look thinner but it couldn't have been that bad, could it? The clothes I was wearing weren't even my own. It wasn't easy to judge if I had lost weight, not to mention the simple fact that I hadn't been paying attention to it. It wasn't like I could do anything about it. I ate when there was food and when there wasn't, I didn't.

With all our traveling and the little we'd had, it was definitely possible I'd lost a few pounds. It was strange, though, because I didn't often feel hunger. It was almost as if I'd reached a point where I could survive on very little. My body had adjusted somehow. Or maybe that was all in my head.

"Hold up," Nick said as he and Bronx caught up to Carol Ann and me. "We haven't decided yet."

"No," I said trying to hide my heavy swallow. "It's fine."

"That-a-girl! You'll see. I promise you won't regret it," Carol Ann said waving her hand over her head. "This way folks!"

TWELVE

The air was crisp as we walked toward Carol Ann's house. It had been a long walk but when we reached her property, I didn't even see it at first.

She pointed ahead and I saw the wooden building hidden deep in a group of trees. The home itself was surrounded by a tall, locked fence.

"My husband insisted on this intricate locking system. Half of it doesn't work because of the EMP we experienced," Carol Ann said pushing the gate open. She gestured for us to make our way through even though our feet moved apprehensively. "It all seemed so silly because if someone wanted to get over the fence, I'm sure they could find a way."

"The high voltage sign might scare people off," I said following her across the lawn to her front porch.

"It might. But if they're using their brains, they'll know it's just a scare tactic." Carol Ann tapped her finger on the side of her forehead. "My husband thinks one day he can get it working again."

"Oh, really?" Nick asked.

"That's what he thinks. I think he's crazy," Carol Ann said as she opened the locked front door and walked inside. She ran her hands up and down her arms as she walked toward the fireplace at the far end of the large room.

The home was gorgeous. Immaculate. Carol Ann had kept it tidy and all of the furniture looks as though it had barely been used.

"Please, please, have a seat," she said. "I want you all to make yourselves at home." Carol Ann had a fire going in less than a minute. "I'm so glad you all decided to come with me. I was so lonely here by myself and losing my mind without my husband here."

I didn't like to hear that word. Crazy.

Carol Ann sat down in a rocking chair near the fireplace. She picked up a long afghan she was nearly finished crocheting. She noticed me looking at her quick-moving fingers.

"Do you know how to crochet?" Carol Ann asked.

"A little," I said. "My grandma had taught me many years ago. I can single and double crochet but anything beyond that I consider advanced. I made a hat once."

"Oh, I can teach you! These blankets might not look like much but they can keep you warm on a cold night. They could save a life." Carol Ann didn't even have to watch her fingers as they expertly moved down the row. It was clear she'd been crocheting for years.

I smiled at her but the last thing I felt like doing was taking lessons on how to crochet. It was the end of the world and I had a far too much to worry about.

"Go on, have a look around. I don't mind. I'd give you a tour but I don't have the energy. Help yourselves to whatever you'd like in the kitchen. I'd prepare something myself but my joints are killing me." She cocked her head to the side and paused her stitching for a moment. "Arthritis and gout... had to cut back on my meds."

"Sorry to hear that," I said. "Don't worry though, I can prepare something for everyone."

"You can? That would be lovely," Carol Ann said and instantly her fingers started moving again. If

I pulled the hook out of her hand, I was sure her fingers would continue to move in the same motion. "Oh, and dear, please pick out a bedroom upstairs for each of you. There are several to choose from."

"Um, okay," I said glancing up the stairs. Bronx followed me as I walked out of the living room and down the short hallway. If Carol Ann wanted us to explore and make ourselves at home that was precisely what I was going to do.

The first floor had a large living room with a fireplace, a bathroom, a huge kitchen, and a fancy dining room. At the back of the fully-stocked pantry was a door. I looked over my shoulder at Bronx before opening it.

My eyes narrowed at the staircase that stretched downward. I stepped down the first couple steps attempting to take a peek.

"Gwen!" Bronx whispered. "What are you doing?"

"She said we could make ourselves at home," I said in a quiet voice. With each step I took down, I became more and more surprised at what I was seeing. It was some kind of panic room of sorts... or maybe it was an underground bunker.

The first section of the room was almost an exact replica of the living room upstairs. I was going to keep looking but Bronx grabbed my arm and pulled me back up the stairs.

"Did you see that?" I asked.

"Yes," he said his voice rippling from his nerves. "When she said to make yourself at home, I don't think that meant she wanted you to snoop."

"But this place is perfect," I said. Brightness radiated from out of my eyes and I was sure Nick saw it as he and Molly came into the kitchen.

"Perfect for what?" Nick asked.

My eyes widened more, the dryness scratched my eyelids when I blinked. "Perfect for our hideaway. We need this place, Nick. We'll never find anything better than this."

Nick narrowed his eyes at me. It looked as though he thought I had lost my mind.

"There is a bunker down there. It's amazing," I said keeping my voice low. I didn't want Carol Ann to know how at home I was making myself. "We are secluded and the supplies are endless."

"Well, that's not entirely true. They will come to an end," Bronx said.

"But not for a very long time," I said biting my lip in an attempt to control my excitement. "And there is even more downstairs. This is it. I just know it is."

Nick shook his head as he waved his hands

around the kitchen. "This is not it. I wish it were but it's not."

My forehead wrinkled at his words. "How can you say that? Look at this place! There is that town not far off where Carol Ann's husband goes to get supplies. How are you not seeing what I'm seeing?"

"Because I'm seeing something you're not. Something you're missing," Nick said.

"What? What am I missing?" I asked with my hands on my hips.

"That this place... is already taken," Nick said with his eyes narrowed.

"Well... Well...," I stammered. "I know that! But I think she'll let us stay here. She seems awfully lonely."

Nick shook his head. "She might but lonely doesn't mean she's ready to live with strangers. It's not like she's going to let us take over her home."

"That's what you think," I said but after a pause, I sighed. "Fine. You're probably right. I guess I just got excited. It was a stupid idea. Forget it."

"It's not a stupid idea," Bronx said.

"Not at all," Nick added. "But we can't just take over. That's not who we are."

I shook my head and sighed. Not once had I suggested we take the place from her. I'd only meant that we could coexist in her space. We could stay with her and work together. All she did was crochet and worry about her husband but they were right, I couldn't just assume she'd want us to stay long term.

It wasn't like we could just take over the place and run it how we wanted to. It wouldn't be right even though that was the kind of world we lived in. No one else would think twice. There were others who'd probably shoot Carol Ann between the eyes for this place. But we weren't those people. We weren't going to be those people.

"You guys should see the bedrooms upstairs," Nick said clearly trying to change the subject.

"Oh?" I asked letting him. It wasn't like I had any more to say on the matter anyway. I was bummed because it seemed perfect and it was going to be awfully hard to walk away when the time came.

Bronx nudged me with his elbow and raised a brow. "Should we go check out the rooms before we eat?"

"Sure," I said sounding far less enthusiastic about the bedrooms than Bronx did.

Carol Ann didn't even look up at us as we walked through the living room and up the stairs. Everything about the home was inviting. It even smelled good. There was a faint smell of cookies being baked in the oven. A smell that reminded me of my grandma.

The first door at the top of the stairs was half-open. I peeked in and saw Christian sacked out on the bed. His leg was hanging off the side as if he'd just made it to the bed before passing out. The position of his head made it hard to tell if his eyes were closed or if he was just staring blankly up at the ceiling.

Bronx shrugged and grabbed my hand. He jerked his head to the next door and I noticed the small number nailed to the middle of the wood.

"What do you think that's all about?" I asked.

His eyes narrowed as he reached out and touched the metal number. He took several more steps down the hall and pointed at the door. "This one had one too."

Soft steps padded up the stairs behind me. Molly was making her way up the stairs shaking her head.

"That one's ours," she said pointing at the door I was standing next to.

"Okay," I said scrunching up my nose at her. It wasn't at all like I cared. Any bed was far better than sleeping on the ground.

"If you were wondering, Nick and I are good again. We talked," Molly said as she stepped by me.

I offered her a tight-lipped smile. "That's good I guess."

"It is." Molly grinned. "It really, really is." Her eyes filled with so much love it almost oozed out of the corners. "Oh, and Nick started making some food."

"He didn't have to do that. I was going to after I finished looking at the rooms," I said doing my best to hold in my annoyance.

Molly shrugged and stepped into the room. Her fingers tightly gripped the side of the door. "He wanted to help."

She didn't say anything more before shutting the door.

THIRTEEN

Bronx and I selected the room across the hall from Molly's. There was a king-sized bed with a massive headboard against the wall. Red and black striped curtains hung over the only window in the room.

In the corner of the room was a gorgeous wooden desk. My fingertips glided over the silky-smooth varnish stopping at a binder at the end of the tabletop.

I flipped open the cover and the beautiful calligraphy writing on the front page. The numbers on the doors suddenly made sense.

"This place was meant to be a bed and breakfast," I said holding up the binder.

Bronx leaned his head forward for a second

before resting it back down on the pillow. "That doesn't explain the bunker."

"Maybe they just wanted to be far away from everything else," I said setting the binder back down on the table. My fingers touched the writing as I read it out loud. "A home far, far away from your home."

"Not a very catchy slogan," Bronx said.

I looked around the room. It was gorgeous. The whole building was. It must have cost a fortune to build.

"Maybe they didn't need it to be. I mean, look at this place," I said. "This is the perfect weekend getaway for almost anyone."

"If you like staying in a bed and breakfast," Bronx muttered.

"You wouldn't?" I asked.

Bronx lowered his head but kept his eyes on me. "I would if you wanted me to but otherwise, no, not my style. When I want to get away, I don't want to have to socialize. I'd rather be in a falling apart cabin in the wilderness, anything, as long as I was alone actually getting away from whatever it was that I wanted to get away from."

"Sounds nice to me. I just didn't know that about you," I said biting my lip. "I guess I don't really know a lot about you."

"What do you want to know?" Bronx asked.

"Anything?" I asked with a smirk.

Bronx leaned forward. "I don't want to have secrets from you. I'll answer anything."

"Oh boy, there is probably a lot I don't want to know," I said.

"Come now, what kind of man do you think I am?" Bronx said getting to his feet. He walked slowly toward me, his eyes glued to mine.

I knew he was a good man. A very good man. He had a heart as big as the universe but at that moment, he looked like he wanted to do bad things. Very bad things... to me.

Bronx's took my hand into his. He traced small circles into the back of my hand causing a cool shiver to run down my spine. The look in his eyes had my heart racing and the room spinning.

I brought my lips to his hoping the pressure that was building inside of my body would be relieved. His warm, silky lips only increased the desire building inside of me.

My heart knocked at the inside of my chest echoing inside my head. Only it wasn't my heart knocking... someone was at the door.

"Yo! Wake up! Dinner is ready," Nick said pounding the side of fist hard against the door.

Bronx pulled back. His eyelids were heavy with passion.

"I could tell him to go away," Bronx said in a deep voice that sent heat racing to my cheeks.

My fingers dug into the front of Bronx's shirt as I pulled the fabric into my fist. "No...," I said swallowing hard. "We should go."

"Are you sure?" Bronx said. "Who knows when we'll get a chance like this again?"

"Is that your new line?" I teased.

"It should be," Bronx said.

I shook my head and smiled at him. "No, you don't need a line."

I leaned forward and pressed my lips to his again. I held them there for a long moment, holding him close.

"At least you don't with me," I said as I took a slow step back. I turned but I didn't let go of his shirt. "Come on."

Bronx stomped after me with a groan. He didn't want our time together to end so quickly... so abruptly. Neither did I but I also didn't want Nick to keep pounding, nor did I want the others talking about what was going on behind our closed door.

It wasn't that I was embarrassed, in fact, that would be far from the truth. Bronx was hot and I knew how incredibly lucky I was but it just wasn't anyone's business what was going on between us.

When we got downstairs, Carol Ann wasn't in her rocking chair. She was sitting at the head of the table with a bowl of steaming hot mashed potatoes and two beef sticks in front of her.

"Ah, there you are. Please join us," she said with a bright, cheery smile.

Bronx pulled out my chair, and I could feel all of their eyes on us, especially Molly's. The look she was shooting at me was filled with jealousy.

"Making us look bad here, man," Nick said with a smile that didn't show in his eyes.

"Sorry," Bronx said. He leaned close to my hear as he lowered himself down next to me. "I'm not even a little sorry."

I bit my lip so I wouldn't smile. "So, Carol Ann," I said clearing my throat. "You ran a bed and breakfast?"

Carol Ann shook her head. "Never got the chance. My husband and I were a week away from opening when the sky turned red. A damn shame we never got to open up this place. It was our dream for more than fifteen years."

She looked down at her food and folded her

hands. Carol Ann didn't have anyone join her as she whispered Grace.

"Amen," she whispered loudly before picking up her fork. "This looks wonderful. Thank you so much for preparing this. I would have done it myself but ever since Dick left, I just haven't been myself. I hope you can forgive me for being a terrible hostess."

"Don't give it another thought. I don't blame you one bit," I said. "I'd be a mess."

"Are you two married?" Carol Ann asked looking at Bronx for a second before shifting her gaze back at me.

"Us?" I said shaking my head. "Nooo."

Bronx narrowed his eyes at me. "You make it sound like that would be a bad thing."

"Oh, no, of course not. I just never gave marriage much thought," I said. When I shyly looked up, my eyes connected with Nick's.

"How come?" Carol Ann asked.

"I guess, I just never saw a marriage work out." My lips pressed together tightly as heat surged to my cheeks.

Carol Ann didn't give me any expression that revealed what she was thinking. "Dick and I were married just after high school. He was my first love and he will be my last."

"That's very romantic," Molly said clasping her hands together, and she leaned forward slightly. She looked at Nick out of the corner of her eyes. "We're not married either."

"I didn't think so," Carol Ann said and Molly turned. She glared at me momentarily letting more of that jealousy seep out. "But we will be... one day, right Nick?"

"That's right," Nick said sliding his hand across the table.

Carol Ann clapped her hands together. "That's lovely. If Dick were here, he could perform the ceremony."

"I'm not sure we're ready for all that just yet," Molly said. "We only first started talking about it."

Nick straightened his shoulders as he avoided my eyes. "With how things are out there, it's not our first priority."

"Ah, yes," Carol Ann said shaking her head. "Luckily, in here, I haven't experienced much of all that. Dick and I have been quite safe. He'd put that fence up for privacy reasons but it's turned into a security fence."

"Yes, this place seems quite perfect for what's going on out there," Nick said.

"Why do you have the basement set up the way you do?" I asked.

Nick's gaze stabbed at the side of my head like I was being poked by a hundred needles. I wished I could take back my question.

"That's Dick's doing. He insisted we build a bunker when we had this place designed. He'd always been worried about the end of the world. A prepper and thank goodness he was. It almost seemed as though he was excited when the sky turned red," Carol Ann said shaking her head. "Boy oh, boy, did he like telling me that he had been right."

Christian stood abruptly. There was sweat beading up at his temples, and his hands were shaking.

"Excuse me," Christian said. He stared at the center of the table for a long moment before he turned and left the room.

The sounds of him moving quickly up the stairs filled the air. Carol Ann's fork stopped moving only for a second. I wondered if she knew what was going on with Christian. Could she tell? Maybe she just assumed he was ill. Either way, she didn't ask nor did she comment on the matter.

It was a pleasant meal but it was strange eating with Carol Ann. For the most part, she acted as if nothing was different. It seemed as though it was a coping mechanism but I wasn't about to judge how anyone dealt with what was going on outside her home. Maybe it was just easier to pretend nothing was happening.

Bronx and Nick stood at the window after dinner. They quietly discussed how they were going to handle keeping watch. Nick suggested that they don't bother.

Carol Ann and Dick had been here since every-thing happened and we were their first visitors. It wasn't like we would have found the place on our own. The only reason we knew where it was located was because Carol Ann brought us to it.

I watched Carol Ann shaking her head as she crocheted. I knew she was listening in on their conversation even though they were trying to keep their voices low enough so that she didn't hear.

"Well," I said clapping my hands softly and awkwardly. "I'm off to bed."

"Good night, dear," Carol Ann said without looking up from her rapid stitches.

"Night," I said bobbing my head.

Bronx turned and grabbed my hand. He pulled me to him and placed a kiss on my cheek. "I'll be up soon."

"Take your time," I said with a tight-lipped smile. "I'm exhausted."

"Is that code? Like saying you have a headache?" Bronx whispered in my ear.

I shook my head and smiled as I squeezed his hand. "No. It's just a fact. See you upstairs."

I walked slowly up the stairs listening to the moans and groans coming from Christian's room. My hand touched the wooden door frame as I leaned in to take a peek.

Christian was lying on top of the covers. Sweat was dripping off his brow and he was shaking as if he were lying in a snow bank.

I turned and look back down the stairs. Nick and Bronx's whispers had vanished.

My shoulders dropped with a heavy sigh as I looked down at my moving feet. I was going into Christian's room and I didn't know why exactly. It wasn't like I knew him very well but I hated to see him suffering.

I took a book off of the shelf in his room and sat down in the chair. My eyes tried to focus on the words on the page.

"What are you doing?" Christian said through his uncontrollable shivers.

I swallowed as my jaw stiffened. "You shouldn't be alone. Not at a time like this."

"Why?"

"I think you know why."

"No," Christian said shaking his head. "Why would you do that for me?"

I flipped the page even though I hadn't read a single word. "I've been through this before with someone I care about. You might need me."

"I've been through this before," Christian said his eyes rolling back slightly. "Alone."

I nodded. "Well, this time you don't have to be alone."

FOURTEEN

A bell rang and I jolted upright. I'd fallen asleep in the chair in Christian's room.

His head was on the pillow and tilted to the side. I watched his chest to make sure he was still breathing.

His chest rose and I quickly stepped out of the room. I didn't want me or the bell to wake him.

Bronx stepped out of our room at the same moment. He was buttoning his pants as he narrowed his eyes at me.

"If I were a jealous man, I'd probably ask a lot of questions about you coming out of Christian's room," Bronx said.

"Good thing you're not a jealous man," I said

with a playful smile. He cocked his head and kept his eyes on me. I knew he was waiting for some kind of explanation. I crossed my arms and looked away from him. "I just didn't want him going through that alone."

"You're such a caring woman," Bronx said wrapping his arms around me. He placed a kiss on my lips but I quickly pulled back. "Something wrong?"

I shook my head. "Not at all."

"Do I have morning breath?"

I chuckled. "No, well, maybe but I didn't notice. I just didn't want that bell to ring again."

"What was that about?"

"I don't know. Let's go find out."

We walked down the short hall toward the stairs. I noticed that Nick and Molly's room was empty.

When we got downstairs, there was a big breakfast on the table. Nick and Molly were sitting next to each other leaning close to one another whispering and smiling.

"About time," Nick said. "Carol Ann was just about to ring the bell again."

"Maybe I should," Carol Ann said stepping into the room. "Your friend still isn't down here. Maybe he didn't hear it."

"He's sleeping," I said. "Christian needs the rest."

Nick looked at me as all traces of a smile fell off of his face. "How kind of you to care."

"Of course," I said pressing my lips together. "I've taken care of people with his illness before and who knows, maybe I'll have to do it again."

The air in the room tightened like a stretched rubber band. If it were pulled any further, it would no doubt snap.

"I'll make a plate for him," Carol Ann said. "You can bring it up when you're finished."

"Sure, but I'm not sure he'll eat anything," I said as Bronx pulled out my chair.

Nick turned to him. "Are you going to do that every time we sit down at this table?"

"If I want to," Bronx said.

Nick stared at him and with the building tension in the room, I was almost certain Bronx was staring right back at him.

"Thank you," I said turning and smiling at Bronx. He looked away from Nick and down at me. I patted the seat next to me. "Sit."

Carol Ann loudly placed a bowl down in the middle of the table. Her eyes darted between Bronx and Nick.

"Dig in," Carol Ann said as she sat down at the head of the table. It sounded more like an order than a request. She scooped what looked like eggs onto her plate.

"Looks delicious," Molly said. "What are these?"

"Powdered eggs," Carol Ann said. "Just as good as fresh eggs if you ask me. Go on now, eat up."

We ate in silence. Bronx took a second helping of the eggs, shoveling them into his mouth as if he hadn't eaten in weeks.

He caught me watching him and smiled. "They are amazing, Carol."

"Thank you. It's Carol Ann," she said sourly.

"My apologies, Carol Ann," Bronx said.

"Oh, think nothing of it," she said waving her hand at him. Carol Ann pushed her plate forward and folded her hands. She placed them on the table, leaning forward slightly. "So, Nick, I have something I've been meaning to ask you."

Nick chewed and swallowed a big bite of food. "After these eggs, you can ask me anything and I just might do it."

"That's what I'm hoping," Carol Ann said. She drew in a slow breath and her eyes stopped on Molly. They slowly moved until they connected with my eyes. "Do you think we could talk in the kitchen?"

"Um, sure," Nick said brushing his hands together before placing them on the edges of the table. He pushed himself to his feet and waited for Carol Ann to lead the way.

"I'll clean up," I said and Bronx nodded.

Molly glanced toward the kitchen. "Need help?"

"No, that's okay. Thanks though," I said and I stood there waiting until they both left the dining room. I was pretty sure Bronx already knew that I planned to eavesdrop.

I stacked the plates quietly and then took a step toward the open doorway that led to the kitchen. My breath wavered as I leaned back against the wall trying to position myself so that I could hear them.

"I have a map," Carol Ann said. My brow wrinkled with confusion. It seemed as though I had missed part of their conversation.

"I don't know, ma'am, it just seems to risky," Nick said.

"It won't take long." Carol and sucked in a deep worried breath. "Please, I can't make it that far myself."

There was a long pause. "I wish I could go and find him for you, really I do, but I can't leave Molly or my sister. They need me."

"I can take care of them. They'll be safe here,"

Carol Ann begged. "It's less than twenty miles. You'll be there before you know it."

"How do you expect me to find him?" Nick said.

"I'll tell you where to look," Carol Ann said. "There are certain places he goes. Please. You're my only hope at finding my husband."

Nick forced out a cough. I leaned over and saw him running his fingers through his hair.

"I'm really sorry, Carol Ann, but I'm going to have to decline. If things were different, I'd give it more thought but with things how they are, I can't. I hope you can forgive me."

"Oh," Carol Ann said in a voice that hadn't sounded like her own. "I wish... I wish... excuse me."

The floorboards creaked with her movements. I barely had enough time to grab the plates and pretend I hadn't been at the door listening.

I quickly pasted a smile onto my face but Carol Ann didn't look up as she zoomed by me. It didn't even seem as if she knew I was there.

I brought the dishes into the kitchen and looked over at Nick. He was tightly gripping the countertop as he leaned forward with his eyes down. His body gently rocked back and forth.

"What was that all about?" I asked.

"She wants me to go out looking for her

husband," Nick answered as he turned and leaned back against the countertop. He crossed his arms and shook his head without looking in my direction. "I can't do that. I can't just leave you guys here."

"Right," I said.

Nick pressed his palm to forehead and groaned. "But I feel terrible about it."

"That's the cop in you speaking. You want to help her," I said setting the dishes down inside of the sink before covering the drain and pouring in some clean water from the jug beside the sink.

"What if I could find him?" Nick said.

I shook my head as I scrubbed one of the dishes. "What are the odds of that? It's more likely you'd get yourself killed."

"I'd be fine. It's you and Molly that I'd be worried about," Nick said.

"We'd be fine," I said even though I didn't want him to leave. The last thing I wanted was for any of us to get separated with the horrible people that were out there.

"Well, it doesn't matter," Nick said as he headed toward the doorway. "I told her I wasn't going to do it."

I set the clean plate down in the drying rack and turned to him. "Yeah, she seemed pretty upset."

"She'll be okay," Nick said. "She probably went off to ask Bronx if he'd do it."

My stomach sank down to my feet. Would she really do that? Would he go?

The dishes would have to wait. I dried off my hands and went to look for Bronx.

FIFTEEN

I t was about five hours later when Carol Ann came out of her room. She grabbed her crochet project and sat down in her rocking chair.

The fire was dwindling and no one had bothered to add another log. Bronx and I were on the sofa, I was so close to him I had practically been on his lap. I scooted over when Carol Ann glanced up at us for a second from her work.

Earlier, after Carol Ann had her discussion with Nick and left the kitchen, I'd found Bronx staring out of the window. I told him what she'd asked of Nick and was pleased to find out that she hadn't asked him.

Bronx, of course, was curious why she didn't think he was up for the task. I told him that Nick had probably informed her that he'd been a police officer. It was something he liked to tell people. It always had been.

Molly came into the room and stretched her arms over her head. She yawned loudly before flopping down into a recliner. Her complexion turned pale and she placed her hand on her stomach.

"Are you okay?" I asked softly.

"Yeah." Molly smiled. Nick was next to her in a second placing his hand on her shoulder. "A brief moment of queasiness. It already passed."

"You sure?" Nick asked.

Molly patted his hand. "I promise. I'm good."

"I should go check on Christian," I said pushing myself to my feet. Bronx caught my hand and tugged back at me. It was a half-hearted attempt to pull me back down on the sofa next to him.

Carol Ann cleared her throat and set her work down on her lap. "Before you leave, I need to tell you all something. Please have a seat."

I sat back down and Nick lowered himself on the edge of the sofa next to me. He was leaning forward slightly with his hands clasped in front of him.

"I'm sorry to have to inform you but I think it's best if you all leave in the morning," Carol Ann said.

"Oh," Molly said wrapping her arms around her middle.

Nick turned sharply and looked at her in the chair. She caught his gaze and held it for a long moment before looking down.

"That storm is still hanging on the horizon," Nick said. I wondered if he had the same sinking feeling I had. "Would it be alright if—"

"No," Carol Ann said sharply. "I think it's best you be on your way."

It was hard to keep my breathing steady. I could feel panic rising up from me feet pinching at every nerve.

Nick held up his palm. "Look, Carol Ann, if this is about—"

"This isn't about anything," Carol Ann said firmly.

Nick took his eyes off of Molly and focused them on Carol Ann. He swallowed hard. "Because I was thinking about what you asked."

"What did she ask?" Molly scrunched up her nose as if she smelled something rotten.

"No," Carol Ann said shaking her head. "I shouldn't have asked that of you."

"It's totally fine," Nick said. He exhaled slowly. "And I'm going to do it for you."

Molly stood. "Do what for her? What's going on, Nick?"

"Carol Ann needs help finding her husband. She has a good idea where he might be," Nick explained.

"Oh no, Nick, you're not going," Molly said. "You know I need you."

"It'll just be a few days," Nick said.

Carol Ann stood and waved her arms wildly. "It was too much of me to ask. I shouldn't have done that. Put it out of your head."

"It's no trouble," Nick said calmly.

"What do you mean it's no trouble?" Molly asked her voice squeaking at the end of her sentence.

"We'll talk about it later," Nick said glancing at Molly.

Molly opened her mouth but quickly snapped it shut. She crossed her arms and stomped out of the room.

"Will you two excuse us?" Nick said sharply.

"Um," I said holding the word.

"Sure," Bronx said taking my hand and pulling me up the stairs.

I was dragging my feet trying to listen but Nick wasn't talking. He was waiting until he couldn't hear us walking anymore.

I wasn't sure how much time had gone by before

I heard the stairs creaking. Nick didn't come to talk to Bronx and me, he went into his room with Molly.

Bronx shook his head when I started to walk toward the door. I wanted to hear what he was saying even though I already had a bad feeling. Bronx didn't stop me from leaving the room.

I walked over to their door which wasn't completely closed. Molly was softly crying. I leaned in closer and saw her sitting on the side of the bed with her face in her hands. Nick was pacing back and forth with his head down. Neither of them saw me standing there.

"I'm sorry Molly, but I have to do this," Nick said.

"You don't have to," Molly said almost completely inaudible.

Nick knelt down in front of her and took her hands into his. "I'm doing this for you. For us."

"You're doing this for you."

"If I don't go, she's going to make us leave. We can't give this place up at least not yet," Nick said.

"She's not going to let us stay here for months and months anyway," Molly said. "If you don't find her husband, she'll probably make us leave."

Nick nodded as he stood. "It'll buy us a little

time. I need to talk to Gwen and Bronx. Will you be all right while I'm gone?"

"Gone now, or gone looking for Dick?"

"Both," Nick said before placing a kiss on the top of her head. "You're going to be okay. We'll get through this. We can get through anything right?"

Molly sighed. "Yes."

"I'd do anything for you. Remember that," Nick said and he turned toward the door.

I took large soundless steps back to my room. I wasn't sure I was going to make it back without getting caught.

"Nick?" Molly said and I kept moving even though I wanted to hear what she was going to say. But I had to keep going because it might be my only chance at getting into the room without being seen.

Bronx was on the bed looking up at me with half-closed lids. "What's going on?"

"Shh! He's coming," I whispered.

"Were you caught?"

I shook my head. "I don't think so."

There was a knock at the opened door and Nick leaned in. "Can I come in?"

"Sure," I said. "What's up."

I had my back to him but I could sense Bronx's

eyes rolling. Nick grunted as he leaned back against the wall.

"I wanted to let you know that I'm going to look for Carol Ann's husband. She's giving me a map and the photo to take with. I should be back in about a week," Nick said.

"Are you sure about this?" I asked.

"I just finished hashing this out with Molly. I don't have the energy to go through it all again." Nick sighed. He looked tired but it was probably from all the emotions he was no doubt feeling. "If I don't do this, she's going to make us leave. I'm buying us time."

I released a heavy sigh. "Well, for the record, I think it's a dumb idea. We could be out there looking."

"Right now, with that cloud still hanging around, I feel a lot more comfortable with you guys in here," Nick said.

"I don't want you out there with that cloud," I said.

"I'll be okay, Sis, but I appreciate your concern," Nick said pulling his shoulders back. Next thing he was going to tell me was that he was a trained professional but he wasn't trained for anything like this. "Mind if I have a word with Bronx?"

I shrugged. "Go ahead."

When I didn't move, he cocked his head to the side. "I meant alone."

"Oh, right," I said. Of course, I knew what he'd meant, but I was hoping he'd start talking before I left. What did he want to say to Bronx that he couldn't say in front of me?

"Close the door behind you, please," Nick said.

Our eyes met and he raised his brow slightly. It was enough of a message that I knew he'd seen me outside of their door.

Of course, he had. He was trained.

I left the room and sat on the floor in the hallway. They spoke so softly I couldn't make out a single word. It was almost as if Nick knew I was sitting outside the door trying to listen in. All I could do was sit there and wait until they were finished talking.

Bronx would fill me in once Nick was out of earshot. At least I was pretty sure he would.

SIXTEEN

I was sitting on the edge of the bed much like Molly had been when I'd been spying on her and Nick. My stomach was spinning and I felt lightheaded.

"Can I tell you no?" I asked already knowing the answer.

"It's better this way. Safer," Bronx said.

"I should go with you guys," I said.

Bronx was shaking his head before I even finished my sentence. "We need you here taking care of Molly and Christian."

"Molly lived in a closet for God knows how long. She can take care of herself just fine," I said.

"They both need you and I don't want you out

there because then I'll be worried about you," Bronx said.

"But why do you have to go?"

Bronx sat down next to me. "I don't have to go. Like I said, Nick told me not to go but with his bum leg... I don't know it'll just be better to have someone watching his back."

"And who will watch yours?" I felt a cold tear trickle down my cheek on the side Bronx couldn't see. It fell down to my pants creating a darkened circle. I placed my hand on top of it so Bronx wouldn't see.

"Nick will," he said.

He trusted Nick but I wasn't exactly sure why. I mean, I guess I knew why. It wasn't like Nick had let him down. He didn't know the Nick from before all of this.

"It's going to be okay," Bronx said. "I promise you."

"You can't make that promise," I said shaking my head.

"I will always find my way back to you," Bronx said placing his finger on my chin and turning me, so I had to look into his eyes.

Certainly he'd see the glassiness... the redness. For whatever reason, I didn't want him to see me cry.

"You need to be here for Molly and Christian. I need to be there for your brother," Bronx said. He placed a kiss on my lips before pulling back. "You know how much I love you, right? I'm not going to lose you."

"Coming back to me isn't something you have control over."

"I will come back to you," Bronx said with a long exhale. "But I wanted to make you promise something."

I shook my head. "Promise what?"

"If something should happen—" Bronx held up his hand "—that delays me, I want you to promise me you'll go to Winnipeg. That's where I'll go to find you."

"I don't know how to find Winnipeg," I said with a frown.

"I'll make you a copy of the map. Gwen," he said placing his hands on my shoulders. He looked deep into my eyes. "You can do it. I know you can. But nothing is going to happen to me."

I looked away from him. "If you believed that you wouldn't need a backup plan."

"It's better to have a plan than to not have a plan." Bronx smiled at me but it seemed forced. "But

I will come back to you. I'll be back before you know it."

"I don't understand why I can't come too," I said feeling another tear welling up.

"You're safer here. Not to mention Nick said you'd want to come along. He said it was important that you stay here and take care of Molly."

"Why do I need to take care of her? She's a grown woman."

Bronx ran his fingers through his hair. "He just said it was important. He said she wasn't as strong as you were."

"Nick said that?" I said narrowing my eyes.

"He did."

"I'm not strong," I said with a hard swallow.

Bronx cupped my face and forced me to hold his gaze. "You are stronger than you think."

"I'm not," I said with an empty chuckle. "If I were strong, I'd be okay with you leaving."

"That's not being strong. Having emotions doesn't make you weak." Bronx's lips curled up slightly at the ends. "I'd be worried if you weren't sad about it. I'm sad about it but I know this is the right thing to do."

"You don't seem sad," I said.

Bronx kissed me. "I'm not very good at showing my emotions. Never have been. But I don't know what I'd do without you. You're what I'm living for you. You are why I keep going day after day in this shitty world."

It felt like a lump was growing in the back of my throat with each of his words. It wasn't the words that were getting to me, it was how he was saying them. I could feel exactly just how true it was. How much he meant them.

"Are you sure about this?" I asked.

"I'm sure. It won't be long," Bronx said.

"How long do I stay here waiting for you to come back? How will I know when I should head to Winnipeg?" I asked.

He shook his head. "I'm not sure... two weeks?"

"That seems like an awfully long time," I said.

"I doubt it'll take that long," Bronx said. "But I wouldn't want you running off and then us showing up a day later. Stay as long as you feel comfortable with,"

"Ah, a guessing game." I frowned. "Oh, how I love guessing games."

Bronx grinned but I could see in his eyes that he was truly sad about the whole thing. I could also see that he believed he was doing the right thing.

"It won't be that bad. You'll see. We'll be back before you know it."

"Too bad it feels like I'm saying goodbye forever. And I've said goodbye forever far too many times in my life."

"This is different," Bronx said.

I shook my head biting my cheek, so the tears didn't stream down my face. "How is this different?"

"Because I'll do anything to get back to you. There isn't anyone or anything that can stop me."

I saw the truth of his statement reflecting in his eyes. Even though I knew there were things that would be out of his control, I wanted to believe him. I was going to do something I didn't know I had the ability to do... I was going to believe him. And that was because I felt the same. There wasn't anything that would stop me from getting back to him if I were in his shoes.

"Okay," I said in a soft voice.

"Yeah?"

"Yeah," I said shaking my head. "Don't get me wrong though, I don't like it."

Bronx sighed. "Neither do I but Nick believes this is what is best for us. Doing what we can to stay here."

I watched Bronx as he got up and walked to the

door. His hand slowly moved up to the lock and he clicked it into place before turning. There was a fire in his eyes and I knew I was the only one that could put it out.

He moved across the floor pulling off his shirt. I was still sad but I couldn't take my eyes off of him. I wanted to feel him, all of him, so that if something did happen, I'd never forget a single thing about him.

My heart pounded inside my chest as I scooted back on the bed. He crawled onto the mattress not stopping until he was above me.

Bronx lowered his mouth down pressing it to mine. The warmth and silky wetness of his kiss heated every inch of my body faster than a raging fire.

I forgot about everything except for how badly I needed Bronx. The passionate look in his eyes told me he was experiencing much of the same.

I wanted the moment to last forever, or at least I thought I had, but when his hand touched my thigh, I wanted nothing more than to wrap my arms and my legs around him. The need for Bronx to take me to the cliff of my pleasure was almost too much for me to hold inside. I felt like I was going to burst.

He kissed down my neck as his hand slid up to the button my pants. When I felt the waistband loosen, my body tensed. The zipper sliding down seemed to echo throughout the room.

"Bronx," I whispered. There wasn't much I could do to stop myself from sounding like I was begging him.

He didn't hesitate. Bronx helped me wiggle out of my pants and before I could even take a breath, I felt him.

I wrapped my arms around him, holding myself as close as I could to his chest. It was like I wanted as much of my body touching his as possible. I wanted us to become one.

"Oh, Gwen," Bronx breathed into my ear. "The things you do to me. I will never get enough."

I knew exactly what he meant. There was just something about him. I knew there wasn't anything that could change how I felt about him.

He was gorgeous. He was caring. And he was perfect for me.

My breathing quickened. Every inch of my body tingled for my release. I wanted it but at the same time, I wanted it to last forever.

"Oh, God," I said breathlessly, unable to hold myself back. I closed my eyes tightly and let him rocket me off of my highest peak. Bronx's body tensed and I could tell he had reached his edge too.

We rocked together... running our hands frantically over every inch of each other. Breathing and whispered our pleasure to one another until we both settled into our peace.

I didn't want to let go. I never wanted to let go. We fell asleep together, wrapped in one another's arms. It was as close to perfect as I could get in this world.

In the early morning, I stared at the ceiling. I didn't want to get up because I knew when I did, it would be time to say goodbye.

Bronx was still asleep next to me. I listened to his slow breaths and let them calm me.

The knock on the door nearly had me jumping out of my skin. I jerked the bed so vigorously the whole mattress shook.

"Huh?" Bronx said pushing himself half-up. He looked around the room as if he expected something to be wrong.

"Someone knocked at the door," I said just before there was another knock.

"Why is the door locked?" Nick asked through the wooden door. "Open up. It's time to go."

SEVENTEEN

I wished there would have been more time to say goodbye. Nick had packed their things and they were gone before the sun was fully over the horizon.

Carol Ann wore a huge smile. She wasn't in her rocking chair like I had expected... she was up and about dusting and polishing every bit of wood inside the house.

"He loves a clean house," she said as she zipped by me for the thirty-seventh time. It was like she expected Dick to come back at any moment.

Molly hadn't come down to say goodbye when the guys were at the door. Christian hadn't bothered to come down either but then, I wasn't even sure if Christian had any idea what was even going on.

I could still see Bronx looking at me with a smile

before he walked out of the door. The image stayed in my head and I worried it was the last time I'd ever see him.

Maybe they were doing the right thing. Perhaps Carol Ann would see that even if they didn't find Dick, they had tried. That act certainly would count for something. I had to tell myself over and over again that what they were doing was for the best.

But still, I wished they wouldn't have left. My stomach had a sourness that felt like it was bubbling up and getting stuck at the back of my throat. The taste was acidic and it felt like it was burning a hole through the front of my neck.

I exhaled as I stood. I would have excused myself from the room but Carol Ann hadn't even seemed to notice I was still there.

The stairs were silent as I walked up them slowly placing my weight on each step. I could hear Molly's sniffs. She was still upset.

I stopped in front of her cracked open door. My hand moved up to push it open but then I let it fall back down to my side. It was better to just give her time.

Christian started coughing and I moved across the hall. I walked into Christian's room without bothering to knock.

He was lying on his side. His lips were dry and cracked.

"Water," Christian moaned. "I need water."

There was a glass half-full on the nightstand from the last time I'd brought him a drink. I picked it up and helped him take a drink.

"How are you feeling?" I asked.

"Like shit," Christian said flatly. He'd taken such a small sip it hadn't done much more than wet his lips.

"Drink more," I urged. His skin was frighteningly pale.

He shook his head but it barely moved because of the pillow. "Later. I feel sick. I need to sleep."

"Okay," I said adjusting the blanket to cover up to his shoulder. I took a step toward the door and the bed springs creaked.

"Please," Christian said his voice hoarse. "Stay with me. I don't want to die alone."

I shook my head. "You're not going to die."

"It feels like I might."

"You won't," I said forcing myself to smile at him. It was hard to do knowing that he was the reason he was going through everything.

"You're too nice to me," Christian said closing his eyes.

I blew out a puff of air as I made my way over to the chair. He was giving me far too much credit.

"I'm sorry... I'm sorry," Christian repeated. His words repeated until they faded away.

The next few days were much of the same. Carol Ann scrubbed and cleaned the house from top to bottom. Christian was miserable as he worked to get the poison out of his body. And Molly spent most of her time alone until the fourth day when I heard her lose the contents of her stomach in the early morning.

I went to check on her just as she was getting to her feet from the side of the toilet. She wiped the sweat off her brow before looking in my direction.

"I shouldn't have done that," she said. "Now I have to clean it up."

"Are you okay?" I asked.

"Stomach bug," she replied quickly.

I crossed my arms as I looked at her. "For how long?"

"A couple days I guess," she said with a shrug. She smiled as she walked by me making her way back to her bed. "I'm fine. Maybe it's just nerves."

"Nerves?"

"I don't know... maybe?" she said. "I wish they were back by now."

I swallowed hard. "Me too. It won't be much longer now."

"Pfft," Molly snorted. "You've been out there. You know just as well as I do that nothing out there is simple."

Molly pressed her hand to her stomach and her complexion turned green. She zipped back to the bathroom closing the door behind her.

That night, Carol Ann prepared a feast. She didn't seem even a little upset when I was the only one to show up when the bell rang.

"They're not feeling well," I explained.

"Oh, that's too bad," she said shaking her head. "After dinner, I can check and see what I have in the way of medicine."

"Thanks," I said not even sure what either of them needed.

Carol Ann scooped some of her soup into her mouth. "I think when my husband returns, he's going to really like having all of you around. We'll get so much more done. It'll be like having staff."

My mouth dropped slightly but I quickly pulled it back up.

"Oh, I didn't mean anything by that, I just meant we'd all be working together," Carol Ann said. "It's a tough world out there, right?"

"Yeah."

"Well, we'll increase our chances at survival if we all stick together." She looked back down at her soup.

I wanted to explain to her that would have been true even if she wouldn't have sent Nick and Bronx to go out looking for her husband. She seemed convinced that her husband was still out there but I couldn't help but think that if he were, he would have found his way back by now. Unless of course he'd been taken. If he had been taken against his will, it wasn't like Nick or Bronx would find him and if they did, they probably wouldn't be finding their way back either.

I shook my head trying to rattle the thoughts away. If I was going to make it through the next few days without losing my mind, I was going to have to stop thinking about what Nick and Bronx were doing out there. I just had to believe they'd come back... that they would be okay.

"Excuse me," I said standing and pushing my chair in. I probably should have offered to help clean up but I needed to get away from the table. I needed to check on Christian to busy my mind with something else. Talking about Carol Ann's missing husband wasn't helping.

"You didn't like the soup?" Carol Ann asked. Her eyes darted around the table. "You didn't touch much of anything."

"Maybe I'm coming down with Molly's stomach bug," I said. "I'm sorry but everything I tried was delicious."

Carol Ann bobbed her head. "Thank you. Go on and get some rest, dear. Hope you feel better tomorrow."

I flashed her a thin-lipped smile and walked out of the room. As I walked by the front window, I noticed that any daylight had almost already vanished. It seemed far too early for night to be setting in.

I looked out the window before opening the front door. I stepped out onto the front porch and crossed my arms as I looked around.

The air was as sharp as a razor blade against the uncovered skin of my arms. The dark clouds that had been sitting on the horizon had moved closer. Some of them were blocking out the sun.

These clouds weren't like any other clouds that floated in front of the sun. They were much thicker and had a dark color to them that was almost a deep shade of purple. In fact, they were so thick and dark that they blocked out nearly all of the light.

I hated that the clouds were moving closer. My eyes scanned the yard hoping to see Bronx and Nick making their way through the trees beyond the fence but they weren't there. The only thing moving was the leaves rustling in the stinging breeze.

I blew out a heavy breath and turned and went back inside the house. Bronx and Nick would have seen the clouds moving... they would be looking for shelter.

Hopefully, they would have found something already. In fact, I was going to tell myself that they had.

EIGHTEEN

Molly and I stood on the front porch. We couldn't even make a guess as to what time of day it was but one thing we were certain of was that even though it looked like the middle of the night, it wasn't.

"I don't like this at all," Molly said wincing as she swallowed.

"Me either." I eyed her as she tightened her jaw and swallowed hard again. "You're not feeling better?"

She shrugged. "Maybe a little. Just nauseated. It's my nerves though, that's all. I hate that they are out there."

"I hated that they're out there and now I really hate that they are out there," I said.

"You're more upset about it?"

I nodded. "I'm worried this is another attack."

"Blocking out the light?"

"Exactly."

"That doesn't sound too bad," Molly said but she didn't sound as if she was sure of herself.

I turned to face her. "Night for God knows how long?"

"Could be worse though, right? You know, like deadly rain or poison clouds."

"They're all bad. We don't know what this darkness is bringing with it. Not to mention plants and trees need sunlight and without plants and trees, there will be no life."

"That'll take time. None of these attacks have lasted that long." She sounded as if she were trying to convince herself more than she was trying to convince me.

We stood there staring at the clouds, watching them slowly inch their way closer to the house. The air was even colder than it had been and it wouldn't be long before the sunlight that still remained was gone completely.

A howling sound in the distance sent a shiver through my body. I wasn't sure if the noise had come from a wild animal or the wind.

"We should go inside," I said.

Molly's eyes moved around nervously. "Yeah... yeah. Let's go."

"What's going on out there?" Carol Ann asked as she threw another log into the fireplace. "It's getting quite chilly in here."

She picked up one of her afghans and wrapped it around her shoulders before sitting down in her rocking chair. Carol Ann looked at Molly for a long moment before turning to me, waiting for a response.

"I don't know what it is," I said shaking my head. "A big thick cloud moving across the sky."

Carol Ann turned her head and looked toward the window. The curtain was closed but the difference in lighting was obvious. "Looks so dark out there. Did I lose track of time today?"

Molly shook her head. "I don't think so. Think it's around lunch time but I'm not sure."

"Doesn't look like it's around lunch time, does it?" Carol Ann asked as her eyebrows scrunched together.

"No, it definitely doesn't," I said gazing out of the window.

"Well, I hope Dick is hiding in one of his usual places," Carol Ann said rocking slowly.

I narrowed my eyes. "Hiding? How will Nick and Bronx find him if he's hiding?"

"Hopefully, they're hiding too until this darkness passes but they have a very detailed map of all of Dick's secret locations," Carol Ann said.

She seemed just as worried about the darkness as I was. But I agreed with her. I hoped that Nick and Bronx were somewhere safe. All I could do, all any of us could do, was to sit back and wait.

"They'll be fine," Carol Ann said with a smile that curled both her mouth and her eyelids. "You'll see."

She picked up her crochet project and her fingers started moving. I wished I had something that I could do that would allow me to zone out and forget about the world outside but there wasn't a project that I could get lost in. Nothing could make me think about anything else.

We didn't spend much more time with Carol Ann. It wasn't like she knew whether we were still in the room or not.

Molly went up to her room and I went to sit with Christian. I dragged the chair over the window so I could keep my eye on the clouds.

It barely moved but the trees started whipping around as if they were each trapped inside of their own personal tornado. The wind screeched and howled reminding me of the noise I'd heard earlier with Molly on the front porch. It hadn't been an animal making the noise, it had just been the wind.

Christian looked a bit better than he had over the last couple days. He was eating a bit of rice and sipping water as he watched me staring out the window.

"Something's wrong, isn't it?" he asked.

"Do you remember that big cloud we saw on the way here? The dark one?"

"Yeah, I think so," Christian said his eye twitching at the corner as if he was trying to remember.

I swallowed hard. "We think it's another attack."

"I knew I shouldn't have left my house," Christian said.

I couldn't help but snort. "Maybe you wouldn't be alive if you were still at your house."

"Who says that isn't better?" he asked.

"It isn't," I said sharply as I turned toward him. There was a time I would have agreed with him but that was before... before I'd met Bronx.

"Won't you ever get tired of traveling? Of running?" Christian asked.

I swallowed so hard it felt like there were hands

gripping my throat tightly. "Of course. I'm sick of running now."

"Then why do you keep going?"

"Because we need to find a place that's safe," I said. "We've been out there long enough to know that you can't just stay anywhere. The others out there are desperate. Evil."

"But this place is safe?" he asked.

I shook my head. "I doubt there is anywhere that is truly safe but this has been the best we've come across since... since the beginning."

"Is that why they left?" Christian asked.

"Yeah." I twisted my fingers together. "The longer we're here, the safer we are."

"Except nowhere is safe," Christian said with a smile.

I squinted at him. "I might have liked it better when you slept more and talked less."

"Ouch," Christian said still grinning as he placed his hand over his heart.

"I'm sorry," I said.

"I know you were only teasing. At least, I hope you were."

My head bobbed as I turned back to the window. The bowl clinked as he set it down on the night-stand. I could hear the bed squeaking as he shifted his weight around to get comfortable. It wasn't long before I could tell by his breathing that he was sleeping.

I didn't go back to my room. Even though Christian wasn't much for company, I didn't want to be alone. I'd tried to keep an eye on what was going on outside but the blowing trees were hypnotic.

When I woke, I had no idea what time it was. It was completely dark.

My neck was stiff from having slept in the chair. I dug my fingers deep into the tissue as I stood and peered out into the darkness.

I couldn't see much of anything. There was movement I knew was the trees swaying but I couldn't see any details. It was nearly pitch black.

There was a light glow coming from the hallway but it didn't do much to light Christian's room. I made my way to the doorway biting my cheek when I kicked the bed frame. It hadn't been that hard but my toe pulsated inside of my shoe.

I kept my hands out in front of me as I stepped out of the room and into the hall. The light from Molly's room lit the hall enough that I could make my way to her door without much trouble.

I was about to turn into her room when she stepped out with a candle in hand.

"Jesus, Molly!" I said taking a step back and placing my hand against the wall. My fingernails scraped against the wallpaper but I couldn't see the mark I'd left behind in the darkness and shadows.

"Sorry!" Molly said. "I was just coming to look for you. What time is it?"

"How would I know that?" I said in a high-pitched whisper.

She shook her head. "It can't still be night, can it?"

"I don't know. Maybe? I fell asleep in a chair."

There was movement downstairs. I froze in place listening to the sounds that I eventually realized were Carol Ann.

Christian was on his feet peeking out of the door. "What's going on?"

"Hey you're alive," Molly said.

"Lucky me," Christian said. The shadows dancing on his face revealed that he didn't believe he was lucky at all. "Why is everyone awake? Is something happening out there?"

I took the candle from Molly's hand. "Not sure. Let's go downstairs and see what we can find out."

NINETEEN

Before we got halfway down the stairs, the glow from the candles and the fire lit the way. Carol Ann was shaking her hand to put out a match when we stepped into view.

"You aren't too cold up there, are you?" Carol Ann asked. "I woke up an hour ago freezing to death. My fingers were so cold I could barely move them."

"It was chilly," I said realizing it once she'd mentioned it. In fact, that could have easily have been the reason why I'd woken in the first place.

"Come on closer to the fire. Warm up," Carol Ann said.

Christian sat down by the fireplace. He looked even thinner than he already had but it was good to see him up and about.

He shivered as he held his hands out to the fire. Christian rubbed his palms together and then looked as though he was trying to move his fingers.

"I think I'm frozen," he said.

"Well, stay nice and close so we can thaw you," Carol Ann said grinning at him. "Nice to see you again."

"Thanks," he said.

Carol Ann sat down in her chair. She pulled a blanket over herself before looking around the room. "Would anyone else like a blanket?"

"No, thanks," I said.

"Sure," Christian said almost too excitedly.

"Take the one off the back of the sofa. That one is made with extra soft yarn. It's one of Dick's favorites," Carol Ann said proudly.

Christian hesitated. "If it's his special blanket—"

"Oh no, I made him one in gray and blue, and another in various shades of green," Carol Ann said. "This one is for guests."

"Um, okay," Christian said as he pulled it off the back of the sofa. He wrapped it around his shoulders and sat back down near the fire.

Silence filled the room. I could hear the wind whistling as it blew against the house making the walls creak like an old bullfrog.

"Sure, is windy out there," Carol Ann said glancing over her shoulder toward the window.

"It is but it's the darkness that has me worried," I said.

"Hmm, yes," Carol Ann said. "I don't feel even a little sleepy for it being the middle of the night."

My eyes widened. "I don't think it's the middle of the night."

"Oh? What time do you think it is?" Carol Ann said looking at me with disbelief in her eyes.

"I'd only be guessing," I said.

"Tell me, what's your guess?" Carol Ann asked.

I chewed my cheek as I stepped over to the window near the front door. It was colder near the door. I squinted as I looked out into the darkness and up at the sky. There wasn't even a tiny bit of light trying to make its way through the clouds above. The moonlight, had it been night, also wasn't there.

"Nine in the morning," I said shaking my head. "It's just a guess, and I could be way off because of how early it got dark last night."

"It couldn't be this dark at nine in the morning!" Carol Ann said looking like she was going to burst out laughing. She looked at the others but they both wore serious expressions.

Molly picked at her fingernails. "Haven't you

seen the other things? The red sky? The poisonous clouds?"

"We've seen them," Carol Ann said as the muscles in her jaw tightened. "They were just oddities."

"They were oddities but they were also deadly," Molly said. "You know how many people died, right?"

"I know," Carol Ann said stiffly. "We don't really talk about it."

It was clear to me that Carol Ann would rather pretend that everything outside her walls didn't exist. That was why she'd been so out of sorts when we'd first met her. It hadn't been just because she was looking for her husband, she hated being out there.

"I'm going to need more wood from outside soon," Carol Ann said. "There's some already chopped but we'll need to chop more. That had been Dick's job. I'm a bit behind since he's been gone."

"I can help with that," Christian said with a shiver.

"Can you?" Carol Ann asked. "Are you sure you're ready?"

Christian shrugged. "I'd like to give it a shot. Besides getting out might help me feel a bit better."

"Well, if you're sure," Carol Ann said and Christian nodded. "I'll try to find some of Dick's winter gear in a bit. I need to rest my legs. The coldness makes my joints ache like you wouldn't believe."

"Winter gear? Is that necessary?" Christian asked.

Carol Ann's eyes widened with her small half-shrug. "Based on how cold it is in here, I can only imagine it's worse out there. And with that wind...," she purposefully shook her torso, "Brrr!"

"We'll worry about it tomorrow," Carol Ann said.

"How will you know when it's tomorrow?" Molly asked. I could tell she was trying to be a smart-ass.

The comment reminded me of something Nick might say in the same situation. I almost chuckled but I was able to bite my lip before it was able to escape.

"I guess we won't," Carol Ann said leaning her head back against her chair. "We'll go when I'm ready."

"Sounds perfect," Christian said.

"Anyone hungry?" I asked stepping away from the window.

Christian turned quickly. His head was bobbing up and down. The shadow on the wall behind him copied his movement.

"I'll go make something for us," I said taking one of the bigger candles off of the table near me.

"Want some help?" Molly asked without moving.

"No, but thanks for the offer. I got it," I said as I left the room but the moment I was alone in the kitchen, I wished I would have accepted her offer.

It felt like the shadows in the kitchen were ghosts dancing around me. All the ghosts of my past were there. Some of them were laughing. Some of them wanted to kill me. I knew it was all in my head but I still couldn't shake the haunting feeling and the noises from the wind wasn't helping.

I decided to make oatmeal hoping it wouldn't take too long so I could get out of the kitchen quicker. It felt like it was taking forever for the water to boil but once it did, I stirred in the oatmeal. I filled each bowl with a large portion and spooned in a large scoop of jam.

I put the bowls on a tray and carried them out to the living room. My feet moved me fast from the kitchen leaving all the ghosts behind to screech and howl after me begging me to come back.

Christian jumped up to his feet when he saw me coming. I thought he was going to take a bowl from the tray, but instead, he took the tray from me.

"Let me help you," he said and set it down on the coffee table. He took a bowl and passed it to Carol Ann and then the next one to Molly.

I picked up my own and sat down on the sofa. The metal spoon felt cold against my fingers as I dipped it into the bowl. I took a bite and even though I'm sure the food was good, to me it was tasteless. My thoughts were getting in the way of my ability to taste the flavors.

I was worried about Bronx and Nick. I hoped they had seen the clouds coming and were able to find shelter in time. The wind would have been too hard for them to walk in, or if they could, they wouldn't be able to go for long. But would they have food?

No one knew how long the darkness would last. If it lasted too long, we wouldn't be okay either but how long I didn't know exactly.

Weeks?

Months?

Years?

I didn't think we had years. It would get cold

without the sun and fast. Hell, it was already getting cold.

Carol Ann was right. We were going to need more wood because the fireplace might just be what keeps us alive.

TWENTY

We'd all slept in the living room. Carol Ann had more than enough blankets that we could create comfortable spots even on the floor.

Christian, Molly, and I all slept on the floor near the fire. Carol Ann had said she was far too old to sleep on the floor. She took the sofa and piled an extra blanket on top.

I was pretty sure that everyone except for me slept longer than normal. The lighting made it difficult to know when night was over and the day began.

I had trouble sleeping but it wasn't because of the cold. It was because my mind wouldn't rest.

There was a tapping sound against the window that caused me to jerk upright. It was slow at first, like someone clicking their fingernail against the windowpane. My eyes moved around the room checking each window, but all of the curtains had been closed.

I should have been keeping watch. If something happened, it would be my fault. It was just that with the wind and the complete darkness I figured that no one would be out there. But what I hadn't considered was that people could still travel with full winter gear and flashlights. Although, if they ran out of batteries, they'd be as good as dead.

The thought made me shiver. I didn't think that Nick had packed a flashlight. Where would he have gotten one? Would Carol Ann have had one in her storage? Maybe in the basement?

I got up and silently made way over to the window. It felt like bugs were crawling over my back as I drew closer to the *tap-tap-tap* sounds. The darkness was awful for so many reasons one of which was that it always felt like there was someone walking one step behind me.

My hand reached out and touched the edge of the rough fabric of the curtain. It was almost as if I could feel every single thread that made up its intricate weave pattern.

"What's going on?" Molly asked from a few steps behind me.

I spun around raising my fist in the air. It took me a second to realize it was really Molly and not some ghost version of her trying to scare the life out of me.

"Don't do that!" I said. The tension in my jaw was so tight I could feel my temples pulsating.

"Sorry. The noise woke me. I saw your shadow... it kind of creeped me out," Molly said as she turned and looked around the room. "Did someone blow out some of the candles?"

"Carol Ann asked me to at some point during the... night or whatever. She doesn't want to run out of candles," I said.

Molly frowned. "Is she planning on that happening soon?"

"I don't think so," I said shaking my head but better safe than sorry.

"I guess." Molly nodded toward the window. "What's that noise out there?"

"Not sure. I was checking when you snuck up behind me."

"I did no such thing."

I placed my hand on my hip. "Well, that's what I call it when you creep up behind someone."

"Ugh," Molly said pushing me aside. She pulled the curtain open and my eyes widened.

There were little, round beads of ice hitting the

window. Each one a tiny little pellet falling from the sky like a miniature bullet.

"Hail?" Molly asked.

"Ice rain," I said.

"What's the difference?"

I shook my head. "I don't know."

I walked to the nearest candle and carried it over to the window. The light reflected back at us making it hard to see outside. I moved closer to the window and placed my hand around my eyes blocking out the light.

"Oh my God," I said. My hand started to shake and I struggled to hold the candle.

The ground was covered in a thick sheet of ice. Everything that was falling from the sky was nearly instantly freezing into a blanket of ice covering everything.

"Maybe it's not as bad as it looks," Molly said placing her hand on top of mine to steady my shaking.

I looked at her, my brow painfully wrinkled. She was the one that would normally be freaking out but she was oddly calm.

"What do you mean? Didn't you see what I saw?" I asked.

"I think so, but we can't see more than what a foot?"

"It's everywhere. I just know it." I tapped the window with my finger. "That cloud blocking out the light is huge and it's dropping this freezing rain below it."

It felt like someone was standing behind me. I turned expecting my mind to be playing tricks on me but when I saw Christian standing there, I let out a tiny scream before I was able to muffle it with my hand.

He narrowed his eyes at me as if I'd done something that offended him. Christian shook his head and gestured toward the window.

"I should get out there... chop that would before the ice is too thick," Christian said. He must have been there listening to everything.

"I'm not sure that's a good idea," I said.

"It would be far worse to run out of wood. The temperature is dropping and with no sunlight, it's going to be like zero degrees in a few days," Christian said with certainty. "We're going to need that wood."

The sofa squeaked as Carol Ann pushed herself up and swung her legs around. "He's right. I'll get the gear and show you were Dick keeps his axe."

Molly relit the candles and I added another log to the fire as they left the room to get ready. I probably should have prepared some food for them before they headed out into the freezing cold but I didn't want to be alone and I didn't want to ask Molly to join me.

I wasn't sure how long it had been before Christian and Carol Ann came back into the living room. The sounds of the falling rain had caused me to get lost in my thoughts and I had to blink several times when they'd stepped into the room.

Carol Ann was wearing what appeared to be pink snow pants and a matching winter jacket. They both wore a dark ski mask over their face and a knit hat on top of their head. Christian and Carol Ann were frightening shadows of themselves.

"How do I look?" Christian asked holding up his hands.

"Great," I said.

"It's quite warm," Christian said. "I might sleep in this tonight... or maybe it's night right now? I lost track. What I mean is—"

"I know what you mean," I said with a smile.

Christian clapped his thick gloves together. "Ready, Carol Ann?"

"Ready as I'll ever be," she said.

"Are you sure about this?" Molly asked cocking

her head to the side as her eyes connected with Carol Ann's. "Maybe I should go with him. You should stay inside."

Carol Ann flapped her hand at her. "Nonsense. That wouldn't be of much help to him since you don't know where Dick keeps his axe."

"I'm sure I could find it with a little direction," Christian said.

"It'll be faster this way," Carol Ann said placing her gloved hand on Christian's arm. "Besides you'll need someone to hold the light. Oh, that reminds me! I need to get the lantern. I'll be right back."

Her snow pants and jacket swished together noisily as she walked toward the kitchen. I could hear things clinking and clanking as she dug around looking for her lantern.

Minutes later she returned carrying what looked like a kerosene lamp filled with some kind of fluid. She lit it and held up it. The room glowed brighter.

"Hopefully, this will be enough light out there," Carol Ann said jerking her head toward the kitchen. "Let's go out the back door." She looked Christian up and down. "You ready?"

"Yep!" Christian said his masked head bobbed sharply.

He turned to follow Carol Ann and I grabbed his

arm spinning him toward me. Christian looked into my eyes blinking several times.

"Are you sure about this?" I asked. "You haven't been well for long. Are you even well now?"

"I'm fine," Christian said patting my hand and then carefully peeling my fingers away from his arm. "Really! Don't worry. I'm good as new."

I swallowed and folded my arms in front of myself, so I didn't reach out for him again. Molly and I followed them to the back door. We stopped several feet away and looked out the window that faced the shed.

The door closed and my body shuddered along with the rattle of the door. Molly looped her arm through mine and squeezed tightly. I pulled back the curtain and watched Carol Ann and Christian slip and slide their way over to the shed.

The lantern lit them enough that I could see the ice rain coating them. Bit of ice dropped off of them crashing to the ground like pieces of thin glass.

Christian worked quickly at first but after several big swings of the axe, his tiredness became apparent. He wasn't ready for the work.

"Hey!" I said breaking my arm free of Molly. I pounded on the glass but they didn't seem to hear me through the noisy wind.

"What is it?" Molly asked with concern heavy on her eyelids.

"He's too tired." I pounded on the window again even though I knew it was no use. "He shouldn't be doing this."

Christian raised the axe up again but this time he missed the log. His grip slipped off the handle and the blade made contact with his leg.

Carol Ann moved over to him. She was looking into his eyes. I thought maybe he was okay because he wasn't moving but then he let out a horrific cry that seemed to shatter the ice around him.

TWENTY-ONE

Molly followed me to the back door. I was about to step out but the coldness pushed me back inside.

Carol Ann and Christian were already at the back door. Her arm was around his back as he hobbled inside.

Blood had soaked through his pants and dripped down covering the front of his shoe. Carol Ann pulled the hat and ski mask off of his head as Molly grabbed a chair.

"Sit," she said.

I couldn't look away from Christian's shock-filled eyes. His pale skin glowed in the darkness like he had already turned into a ghost.

"Get my first aid kit," Carol Ann ordered. "It's in

the cabinet in the downstairs bathroom."

Molly dashed out of the room. Carol Ann looked up at me for a moment as she was helping him out of his jacket. She tossed the clothing into a pile on the kitchen floor.

"Help me get him out of these pants," Carol Ann ordered. She waved her hand in the air frantically. "Never mind, I have to cut them off."

She stood and grabbed a large scissor out of the cupboard. The tearing sounds of the scissors slicing through the fabric sounded loud.

There was blood on the floor. A puddle around his foot. I felt lightheaded. I stepped back and placed my hand on the counter.

Molly was already back in the room handing Carol Ann the first aid kit. She placed her hand on my shoulder.

"He's going to be okay," Molly said with a tight-lipped smile.

I looked at her and blinked. The room came back into focus, and it felt like I was breathing again.

Christian was shivering in the chair wearing only his shirt and boxers. My feet carried me into the living room. I gathered a few of the afghans and practically ran back into the kitchen.

"No!" Caron Ann said holding up her hands.

"Not those. Get one of the bedspreads from upstairs."

I wanted to ask if she was serious but I couldn't stand to see Christian shaking. Carol Ann turned back around and continued patching up his wound.

"It's really deep," she said as she patted Christian's knee. She looked up into his eyes. "But I think you're going to be just fine."

"I think he needs stitches," Molly said.

"Do you know how to do that?" Carol Ann asked with a roughness to her voice.

Molly frowned and looked away from Carol Ann's intense stare. "No."

"Me either. This is the best we can do. We just need to keep pressure on it until the bleeding stops. We'll take turns." Carol and turned sharply and looked me up and down. "What are you waiting for? Go get that blanket."

Christian was still shivering but he looked at me. A softness had replaced the fear and panic that had saturated them earlier.

He smiled at me. "I'm okay, Gwen. It's just a scratch."

"A scratch?" I asked.

"Yeah," Christian said. "A really nasty scratch. This isn't even the worst injury I've had. I fell off a stage once in England. They kept me in the hospital for nearly two weeks. Of course, one of those weeks I don't remember at all."

I wasn't sure if he was trying to make me feel better by telling me the story. He must have noticed the grimace on my face.

"What I'm trying to say is... I'm a lot tougher than I look," Christian said his eyes fluttering rapidly as Carol Ann attached the last bit of gauze with some medical tape.

"Yeah, I know you're tough," I said with a warm grin. "It's just that you only got back on your feet recently."

"And I'll be back on them again soon enough," Christian said.

Carol Ann repacked the supplies into the first aid kit. "Might as well keep this out. I'm probably going to need to replace that gauze soon." She turned to Molly. "Help me get him into the living room."

Molly nodded.

Carol Ann shoved the first aid kit in my direction and shook it until I took it from her. "You carry this."

I swallowed hard but I took the metal box from her. That was all she thought I was good for... carrying supplies and maybe preparing meals.

Although, I'm sure she didn't think my meals were anywhere near as good as her grand feasts were.

I pressed my lips together at the thought. She was wasteful and I was rationing. My way was superior. Let her think what she wants. I wasn't about to let it get to me.

Once we were in the living room, I set the box down on the coffee table and moved to help Christian down into a chair. Carol Ann stepped back and stared at her carpet for a moment.

She walked back into the kitchen and quickly returned with both the lantern and a stack of dish towels. Carol Ann spread them around the floor under the chair. She didn't say it but she was protecting her carpet. Carol Ann didn't want Christian's blood to ruin the carpeting of her B&B.

"I'll be right back," Carol Ann said as she walked toward the kitchen carrying her lantern.

"Where are you going?" I asked.

"Someone's gotta bring that wood in, don't they?" she said. If her tone hadn't been so harsh, I would have offered to help.

The second she was out of the room I knelt down next to Christian. "Can I get you anything? Food? Oh my God, I need to go get that blanket for you."

"First can you guys help me get closer to the fire?" Christian said.

"Sure," I said reaching down to help him up. Molly and I helped him over to the fireplace. I helped him stand until Molly was able to bring the towels over to protect the floor.

She spread the towels around and then we helped him get down. Once he was situated, Molly adjusted the towels.

"I'll run and get that blanket," I said but only made it halfway up the stairs before I realized I needed to take a candle with me to light the way.

When I got back downstairs, Carol Ann was coming in the back door. I heard her stomp her feet several times likely trying to shake the ice off her boots.

She dragged her feet as she came into the living room. Her eyes moved from the chair over to where Christian was lying on the floor. Her jaw stiffened but when she noticed we'd moved the towels, it relaxed slightly.

"I need to rest," she said hobbling as she walked over to her rocking chair near the fire. "That's far too much work for my old bones."

"Where's the wood?" I asked.

"Left it just outside the door," she groaned as she

flopped down in her chair heavily. I started toward the kitchen. "Just let it be for now. It's covered in ice and we've got more than enough inside for a day or two anyway."

I offered her a nod as I walked over the fireplace. Christian smiled at me as I laid down on the floor, pulling the afghan over my body. I should have been making dinner but I needed a rest. Not sleeping had finally caught up with me.

TWENTY-TWO

When I woke, Carol Ann was on the sofa moaning. Molly was pacing back and forth behind her running her hands through her hair.

"What's going on?" I whispered.

"They're not feeling good," Molly said. "I don't know what to do. I gave her water but that didn't help. She doesn't want food."

Sweat was dripping down off of Christian's temples. He looked worse than he had when he was going through his withdrawal.

"Christian?" I said tapping him on the shoulder. He didn't respond in words. All that had come out of his mouth were strange, painful noises. I wasn't even sure if he was fully conscious. I shook him a bit harder. "Christian!"

"They're getting worse," Molly said.

"Why didn't you wake me?" I asked getting to my feet.

I walked toward Carol Ann and placed my hand on her forehead. She was so hot I had to pull my hand back. I looked at the fire as if the answers would show in the flames but all it did was remind me just how chilly the room still was.

"She has a fever," I said walking over to Christian. I already knew before I touched him that I was going to feel the same thing. "Oh, God."

"What?" Molly said wrapping her arms around her middle.

I couldn't answer her. All I could think about was getting their gear out of the kitchen.

Molly followed me as I raced into the kitchen. I opened the drawers even though I wasn't exactly sure what I was looking for but when I saw the oven mitt, I knew that was what I needed.

"What are you doing?" Molly asked as I put a mitt on each hand.

"Stay back," I said holding my breath.

I bent down and picked up their winter gear making sure to keep it as far away from my body as possible. I opened the closet and threw each item in there including the boots that had been left near the door.

"I don't understand," Molly said sounding as if she were near tears.

"It's all contaminated." I shook my hands until the oven mitts fell into the closet.

I closed the door with a hard bang tempted to search for duct tape to seal it shut but the clothing had been lying around for hours. If it were going to make me sick, it would probably have done so by now.

"Contaminated with what?" Molly asked grabbing my arm and forcing me to stop moving about the kitchen. I couldn't help but think there was more I should have been doing.

"She said she didn't bring any wood in, right?"

"Right," Molly said. "Would you, please, explain?"

I let out a heavy sigh. "I think this is another attack. They've been poisoned."

"Poisoned?"

"I've seen this before. Hell, we've been through it before when the sky was red. Didn't you get sick?"

"Yeah.... Okay, well, what do we do for them?" She asked.

I frowned and looked away from her. "There isn't much we can do... we just have to wait."

"Wait?" Molly snorted. "There has to be something we can do!"

"I don't even know if we should take the blankets off of them. It might help to lower their body temperature but it's so cold in there. I don't want them to freeze to death either."

Molly pressed her hands to her forehead. "Let's try. We have to try."

"Okay... okay," I said.

My thoughts drifted back to when Blair had taken care of me. If it hadn't been for her, I don't think I would be here today. It was too bad she wasn't still with us because whatever she had done had done the trick. The only thing I could remember was that she had watched over me... brought me water. But maybe there had been more than that and I just didn't remember.

We didn't have the blankets off of them for more than a few minutes before they started shivering. They couldn't regulate their body temperature.

"It's the poison that was in the freezing rain that's doing this," I said confidently.

"How do you know it's not their fever?" Molly asked.

"Well, it is but what do you think caused the fever?"

She shook her head. "How can you be so sure?"

"I... I just am."

Molly started to pace. "I wish Nick were here."

"Why?"

"He'd know what to do."

"He'd do the same things we're doing," I said but I wasn't sure I sounded convincing.

Molly ran her hands up and down her arms. "We aren't doing anything. We have to do more."

"All we can do is try to keep them comfortable," I said pulling the blanket back over Christian. I watched his eyes darting around underneath his lids. "And try to keep them alive."

Molly dropped heavily onto the chair and broke down into tears. I walked over to Carol Ann and pulled the blanket up to her shoulders.

"What's the point?" she sobbed. "We've lost them."

"We haven't lost them yet," I said.

She shook her head and the tears streamed down her cheeks. "Not them," she sniffed hard. "Nick and Bronx."

TWENTY-THREE

Molly had cried herself to sleep and I drifted in and out for a while keeping my eyes on Christian's breathing. Watching his chest rise and fall slowly hadn't been even a little soothing. I worried with each inhale that it might be his last.

We hadn't blown out any of the candles and I didn't know where Carol Ann had kept the extras. I put it on my to-do list to search for them later. If Carol Ann came to, I wouldn't have to worry about it, because she'd be able to tell me where I could find them.

I sat up and pulled my knees to my chest. The *pat-pat* of the ice rain hitting the window seemed to be slowing significantly but the darkness still remained.

I had to hope that the poison was in the rain and not in the darkness. If Nick and Bronx were still alive, which I had to believe they were, they would have stayed out of the rain. They would have known.

The chair squeaked as Molly shifted her weight. I could feel her eyes on me but I didn't look across the room at her.

"Did you get any sleep?" she asked.

"Not much," I said. "I think the rain is stopping."

"That's good news," Molly said stretching her arms over her head. It was like she woke up as a whole new person. A person that wasn't losing her mind... at least not yet.

Molly walked over to the window but before she was able to pull back the curtain, Carol Ann started coughing. She was at her side before I was able to get to my feet.

"Carol Ann," she said helping her into a seated position. "Are you okay?"

The woman's chest sucked inward and rumbled with each thick cough. Her eyes were still closed.

"Carol Ann!" Molly said louder as she patted her back.

I picked up her glass off the coffee table and held in front of her. "Carol Ann, try to take a drink."

It didn't even seem as if the woman had heard

me talking to her. Her body was doing what it needed to but her mind was still off.

"What should we do?" Molly asked looking as if she was struggling to hold the woman upright.

I stepped up beside her and helped her hold Carol Ann. "Wait for it to pass."

"That feels a lot like doing nothing."

There was an odd sputter from the floor. Christian's cough started slow but it turned into something more aggressive before I was able to even get to him.

"Oh, Jesus," I said as vomit started pouring out of his mouth.

I lifted him as best as I could, hoping he wouldn't choke. They hadn't been eating but even in the dim light, I could tell it was mostly bile coming up.

"Is he okay?" Molly shouted. Her panic had returned.

"I don't know. He's puking."

Somehow, I remained calm even though I couldn't have been more worried that something was really wrong. There was more vomit than I thought possible.

Just when I thought he was about to stop, he started up again. It wasn't long before Carol Ann joined in.

"Oh my God!" Molly screamed. "I can't hold her."

"You have to!" I said still doing my best to hold Christian.

"I can't, Gwen, I can't. I'm not strong enough!"

Christian's coughing and vomiting were slowing but I couldn't leave him. I looked down at him and almost lost the little bit that was in my stomach.

There were dark chunks in the vomit that I almost instantly knew was blood. Christian's body when limp but I was able to ease him back just slightly, so he didn't fall down into his mess.

"Gwen! Please! Help me!" Molly screeched in a high-pitched voice.

I did my best to make sure Christian was okay. He seemed to be breathing albeit slowly and I felt a pulse... just barely.

I dashed over and held Carol Ann's opposite shoulder. There was vomit all over the blanket on top of her legs and splatters on the sofa.

I had to cover my nose and mouth and avert my eyes.

"Carol Ann!" I shouted as if I was trying to wake her from a nightmare. It didn't work.

"Oh God," Molly repeated over and over again. She didn't stop until Carol Ann started choking.

"Carol Ann!" I said shaking her body. If only I could get her to wake up.

I hit her back several times before wrapping my arms around her and trying to dislodge whatever was stuck in her airway free. I jerked her toward me several times but her body just became weaker and weaker. It felt as though I could feel her trying to take a breath.

"It's not working, Gwen," Molly said.

"What do you want me to do?" I asked squeezing her quicker and harder. "I don't know what I'm doing."

"I don't know... I don't know," Molly said unhelpfully.

I felt a change in Carol Ann's body and I stopped trying to help her.

"Don't stop!" Molly said with wide eyes.

I shook my head. "Molly," I swallowed hard, lowering the woman back down even though she was covered in her own vomit. "She's gone... she's gone."

"No," Molly said in a rough voice. "She can't be."

I placed two of my fingers on her wrist. There was nothing. Her lips were a dark brown shade. If we would have had more light, I was pretty sure they would have been blue.

"Oh my God," Molly said taking a step back.

I dashed back over to Christian and felt for his pulse again. My fingers were shaking and I couldn't find it.

"Christian!" I begged into the silence.

I grabbed my hand and squeezed it with my other hoping the pressure would help me steady it. My fingers touched his hot flesh again carefully feeling for the beat.

"Oh God," I said lowering my head as I exhaled all of the oxygen from my lungs.

Molly gasped. "Is he gone too?"

"No. He's alive."

"Oh, thank God," Molly said the words quickly as she dropped down to her knees. "Thank God."

"Don't thank anyone yet," I said. "He was puking blood. And his pulse is weak. Very weak."

Molly covered her mouth with her hand. "What are we going to do, Gwen?"

"We're going to clean up the mess," I said almost throwing up at the idea.

"I mean for Christian."

Tears welled up in the corners of my eyes. "I don't know... I don't know."

"And her... what are we going to do about her?"

My head was down but my eyes shifted upward. Carol Ann merely looked like she was asleep... coated in a thick layer of vomit but asleep.

"We'll wrap her up in a blanket," I said the first thing that came to my mind.

"And then what? We can't leave her in here... she'll start to... decompose." Molly looked down and I wondered if she was thinking about her parents.

They'd been dead in the bedroom where we'd found her hiding in the closet. She'd lived with them in that state. Molly knew better than I did how all that would go.

"We can't take her outside... we can't even push her out the back door at least not until the rain stops," I said looking at Molly.

I was suddenly very worried about what would happen to me if I lost Molly. The last thing I wanted... maybe for the first time in my life... was to be alone.

"Okay," Molly said. "You're right. I can't go near that door. I shouldn't even go near the windows. Maybe I shouldn't have even gone near Carol Ann!"

"You'll be fine," I said even though I wasn't entirely sure. But with our past experiences, the sicknesses never seemed to have been contagious.

"You don't know that." Molly stamped her foot. She tensed up so tightly it looked as if her head was going to pop off. Molly grabbed a candle from the end-table. "Excuse me."

She ran up the stairs leaving me with the mess.

TWENTY-FOUR

I didn't bother to go up and ask Molly for help until after I'd finished cleaning. It had taken me hours although it had felt like days.

I wanted to move Christian to the sofa which hadn't been difficult to clean. Most of the mess had been on the blanket although there had been some that had splattered on the top cushions. I'd done my best to clean the area and covered it with a fresh afghan.

If Carol Ann had still been alive, she would have no doubt been quite angry. But she wasn't alive.

I crept up the stairs slowly. The only thing I could hear was my racing heart.

At the top of the stairs, it felt as though I had entered the Arctic. My hands were so cold I was sure

I could reach out and touch the flame without being hurt. Of course, that probably wasn't true.

"Molly?" I whispered in case she hadn't already heard me approaching.

She didn't respond.

My heart started to pound faster afraid that something had happened. I walked faster looking into the room she had shared with Nick.

"Molly!" I said louder.

I didn't see her but the candle she'd taken was on the dresser. A soft cough followed by a groan came from the bathroom.

My feet carried me faster. I stopped in the doorway just as Molly turned and threw up into the toilet.

"Molly!" I said stepping up behind her. I crouched down next to her and rubbed her back.

Why was she sick? Had I been wrong? Was whatever had been in the rain contagious?

"I'm fine," she said holding onto the wall as she got to her feet.

"You're sick."

"I'm not sick."

I narrowed my eyes at her. "You just threw up."

"It's my stomach. I'm worried."

"Molly," I said trying to grab her arm as she walked by me and back into the bedroom.

The bed creaked loudly as she sat down on the edge of the mattress. I crossed my arms and stood in front of her.

"I'm not sick," she said refusing to meet my eyes.

"I know what I just saw."

"Like I said, I'm worried. I miss Nick."

I shifted my weight and shook my head. She glanced up quickly.

"I miss Bronx too but I'm not throwing up," I said.

"Don't you think my throwing up was different from what happened down there? They were violently sick. I'm pretty sure Carol Ann actually threw up part of her stomach."

She made a point but it still didn't make sense that she was throwing up at all. It wasn't like she missed Nick any more than I missed Bronx.

This hadn't been the first time I found her throwing up in the bathroom. The last time had been before Carol Ann and Christian had gone outside.

"All that down there just turned my stomach," she said as if trying to explain further.

I couldn't stop looking at her. There was something in her eyes. It was like she was keeping something from me. I could tell by the way she would only look at me for a few seconds before looking away.

"I shouldn't say," Molly said.

"Say what?"

"I don't know anything for sure."

"Molly!" I said sharply. "Tell me what's going on."

She let out a quick breath. "I think I'm pregnant."

"What? When? How?" I bit my cheek. I didn't need her to answer that last question. Somehow it had just popped out of my mouth. The last thing I wanted to hear was how.

"I'm pretty sure you can guess how," Molly said without looking at me.

"Is it Nick's?"

Molly turned and glared at me. "Of course, it's Nick's."

"Sorry." It was my turn to look away from her. "Does he know?"

"Yeah, he knows."

I started pacing as the new information sank in. What the hell were we going to do? It wasn't like she was ready to have the baby now but I didn't know the first thing about delivering a baby.

"Then why all that stuff with Christian?" I asked. I wanted to take back the question the second it was out of my mouth.

"Jesus, Gwen. I wasn't sure at the time. My head was a mess. It was a mistake." Molly grimaced. "And really it's none of your business."

"I'm sorry... I'm just kind of shocked." Although I guess maybe I shouldn't have been. "What are you going to do?"

Molly rolled her eyes. "Do I have options? Besides, Nick wants me to have it."

"Well, what do you want?"

"I don't know. I mean, if things were different, I know without a doubt what I'd do but a baby in this world? It just seems cruel," Molly said closing her eyes and exhaling. "Nick says we'll be somewhere safe long before I'm ready to have the baby. He thinks it's going to be fine. He thinks we're going to be a happy family."

Old Nick probably would have run as far and as fast as he could if a woman would have told him he was going to be a father. Suddenly, I wondered if that's why he'd left. Then again, if it had been, he wouldn't have taken Bronx with him.

"But if he doesn't come back...." Molly chewed on her cheek so hard it sucked inward. It appeared as though she was trying to stop herself from crying.

"If anyone would survive, it's Nick and Bronx. He'll find his way back to you, I just know it," I said trying to sound convincing.

Molly shook her head. "I'm glad you think so but I think something happened. They should have been back before the ice rain."

"Maybe they got lost. Neither of them know this area."

"Sure and maybe they won't ever be able to find their way back."

"They'll find their way back," I said.

Molly snorted. "That's assuming they didn't get sick like Christian and Carol Ann. Look what happened to Carol Ann!"

I didn't want to think about Nick and Bronx somewhere puking their guts out. But even if they were, they'd fight like no one else. It wouldn't be the first time either of them had fought off the illness that resulted from one of the attacks. They could do it again.

"I was going to ask for your help but now I'm not so sure," I said changing the subject.

I needed more time to process everything before I said something that could send Molly or myself for that matter spiraling downward. We needed to stay strong... more than ever.

"What do you need help with?" Molly asked.

"Getting Christian onto the sofa."

"Eww."

I chuckled. "I cleaned up."

"You didn't have to do that. I would have helped."

"It's not a big deal," I said with a shrug. "Don't give it a second thought."

"I'm feeling better now. I mean I'm feeling awful but I'm not about to throw up." Molly stood. "Let's go."

"Are you sure? I mean, should you? They're awfully heavy," I said unable to stop my eyes from moving down to her incredibly flat stomach.

Molly cocked her head to the side. "It's fine."

I followed her down the stairs. "You know, maybe it's just stress or from losing weight."

"What is?"

"That you think you're pregnant."

Molly shook her head. She turned to me as we walked into the living room. "Remember when Nick and I were in the trailer? We weren't just talking. I'd found a pregnancy test in the bathroom."

"Oh."

"Yeah. I'm pretty sure."

"You need to eat more," I said.

Molly smiled. "I appreciate you caring."

"I should, right? I'm going to be an aunt."

Not once in my entire life did I ever consider that Nick would have children. I never once thought I'd be an aunt.

Molly's shoulders dropped. "And I'm going to be a mom. How the hell am I going to do that? What if Nick doesn't come back? I can't do this alone."

"You won't be alone," I said shaking my head. "I'll be with you."

TWENTY-FIVE

With a lot of effort and time, we managed to get Carol close to the back door. It was still raining, so we hadn't been able to get her outside. We contemplated just pushing her out of the door but I didn't want Molly anywhere near the rain... not after what she'd told me.

We'd managed to get Christian onto the sofa. He hadn't coughed or puked again, nor had he opened his eyes.

Molly and I had both fallen asleep next to the dwindling fire. There were a few more logs inside the house but we didn't have a lot left.

When I woke, it was so cold in the room I had no choice but to add another log. If the rain didn't stop,

I'd wrap myself in clothing and run out and get a few more. Then again, maybe we couldn't burn anything that had been covered with the poison.

I let out a heavy sigh that caused Molly to stir.

"Everything okay?" she groaned as she sat up.

"Yeah, sorry. I didn't mean to wake you." I said looking at the table next to the chair. We weren't going to need the logs outside. "We'll just burn the furniture."

Molly shook her head. "What are you talking about?"

"I was thinking about the logs. That poison might have soaked into them."

"Does it matter? You can't go out there to get them." Molly's eyes popped open. "Unless it stopped raining. Did it stop raining?"

I shook my head although I hadn't checked. My eyes narrowed as I listened for the little ping noises of the ice tapping against the window pane. I didn't hear anything.

"Maybe it did. I don't know but it doesn't matter. We can't use them but we can use the furniture," I said raising my brow.

"Carol Ann would be pissed."

"What's she going to do about it?"

Molly yawned and stretched before walking over to the window. The curtain hissed as she pulled it back, revealing nothing but darkness.

"Damn," she said. "One of these days I hope to do that and see sunlight again."

"Me too," I said kneeling down next to Christian.

His skin was so pale and his lips were dry and dark. I took his wrist into my hand to check his pulse but when I touched his skin, I felt nothing but coldness.

I stared at his chest waiting for it to rise but it didn't move. My breath caught in my throat making it hard to swallow. I jerked away from Christian and covered my face with my hands.

"Gwen?" Molly said.

"Dammit." I swallowed hard forcing my voice to work. "He's gone."

Molly didn't move. She just stared at the sofa... blinking. "He's... he's dead?"

It was like she couldn't comprehend my words. They didn't seem to make sense to her.

"Yeah," I said. "He's cold. I don't know when it happened."

"The cold killed him?" Molly asked turning to stare at the fire.

"No. I'm pretty sure it was the poison."

Molly seemed as though she'd gotten smaller. "Oh."

She tried not to let her lower lip quiver but trying to stop it only made it worse. I wanted to tell her that everything would be okay, that we hadn't gone outside so we were safe. But I didn't think her thoughts were about us.

And I didn't know if we were going to be okay. Everything just kept getting worse. It was like someone was pulling the thread of my life and slowly unraveling it.

"Nick is going to find his way back to you," I said without thinking. "He knows about the baby. He has something to live for. You know Nick. He's not going to let anything stop him."

A tear trickled down Molly's cheek but she held her jaw steady as she bobbed her head. She wanted to believe me. I wanted to believe me.

* * *

Time ticked by. I wasn't sure how many days had gone but the darkness was still there. I'd broken one of Carol Ann's chairs and I would break another before I'd burn the possibly contaminated wood.

Molly and I didn't go away from the fire for long.

The only time we left was to collect food or if we had to use the restroom.

Every so often, Molly would get nauseated. Sometimes it would pass and other times she'd throw up into a trash can she'd lined with plastic bags she'd found in the kitchen cabinet under the sink.

We were managing to stay alive but we didn't talk much. I knew with every passing minute that Molly was convincing herself that Nick wasn't coming back. She was falling further and further into her own darkness and I didn't know what to do about it.

I tried to talk to her but her answers were short. It was hard to force myself to be positive because I too was struggling, but of course, I couldn't let it show. I had to do it for her and the baby.

"Eat something," I urged when she opened her eyes.

"My stomach hurts."

"That's because you need to eat something."

I shoved a breakfast bar in her direction and she shook her head. My eyes moved around at the small stack of food we'd stockpiled on the coffee table. I picked up the opened box of saltines and passed them to her.

Molly shook her head but then reached out and took them before I was able to frown. She took out a cracker and watched it as she flipped it from hand to hand.

"I can't do it, Gwen."

"It's just a cracker."

She shook her head. "No. Not that. I can't keep doing this."

"What choice do you have?"

"We both have a choice."

"No," I said firmly. "Nick and Bronx will come back. We can't let them walk into that."

Molly looked down. "I wish I could be strong like you but I can't. There is no way I'll ever be able to do this. The darkness has to be worse than the poison."

"What are you saying?" I asked as she stood and walked over to the window. Molly placed her hand on the glass.

The ice rain had slowed but occasionally a drop would fall from a tree or maybe from the sky.

"All I have to do is walk out there," Molly said.

"Did you see what happened to them? Would you really want to do that to yourself? To your baby?" I asked taking a step closer.

"Of course, I don't want to," she said practically

sneering at me. "But I can't live like this. I can't do this without him."

I held up my palms. "Molly, please. Just give it more time. They'll come back, they're just waiting for it to stop."

"They're not alive," Molly said closing her eyes slowly.

"You don't know that!"

"I think if they were still alive, I'd know it. I'd feel him." She turned back toward the window. "If I stepped out there, it wouldn't be long. I'd only suffer for a short time. This," she said waving her arms around, "is worse. This is torture."

I sighed as I ran my fingers through my hair pulling it hard when I got to the ends. She wasn't wrong. It was hard. It was torture. I worried we were going to run out of wood.

If we didn't have the fire, hypothermia would get us. Hypothermia would be far easier than the poison but I didn't want to give Molly any more ideas for ending her life. It was bad enough that I'd have to keep one eye open at all times, so she didn't try sneaking out the back door.

Molly ambled toward the sofa but she didn't sit down. I narrowed my eyes at her. She jerked and moved quickly toward the front door.

"Molly, no!" I screamed as I dashed toward her. I caught her arm just as she reached out her hand toward the doorknob.

"Let me go!" Molly said clawing at my hand with her fingernails.

"I won't!" I grabbed her tighter, holding her with both hands. "If you go out there, you're taking me with you."

Molly released a haunting chuckle. "I'll be saving you."

"I don't want to be saved. Not like that," I spat. "It'll be murder."

"Oh well," she sang.

I knew she didn't mean it. Somewhere inside of her, she believed that if she took me with her, she'd be helping me.

"Please, Molly," I begged.

"No. I can't." She jerked trying to pull herself free. I was stronger. I didn't know how I was stronger but I was.

All of a sudden, she stopped moving. Her eyes widened and she looked down.

I relaxed my grip as I watched her move her hand down between her legs. She held a shaking hand upward between us and even in the dim light I could tell there was blood on her fingers. It had been enough to soak through her jeans.

Tears rolled down her cheeks and her eyes rolled back. I caught her just before she crashed to the floor.

TWENTY-SIX

Molly had fainted. Not because of blood loss but because of what she'd seen on her hand. I'd managed to get her to the sofa without much trouble, placing a towel underneath her.

"Gwen," she said softly, her eyelids fluttering open. "Did I lose the baby?"

I swallowed hard. My heart pulsed harshly inside of my chest. "I don't know."

She looked down at her legs and noticed the towel. None of the blood had managed to soak through.

"I think it stopped," I said.

"Will you help me to the bathroom?" she asked. "I should clean up."

"Yeah, of course," I said offering her my hand.

She took it and I helped her get to her feet. I grabbed a nearby candle on the way to the downstairs bathroom.

We weren't all that far from the fire but the drop in temperature was quite noticeable. It was colder than any winter I'd ever experienced. I turned my back and gave her privacy.

"I'm going to need to change," Molly said shivering. "Let's check Carol Ann's room."

She wrapped a towel around her bottom and I followed her out of the room. We dug through Carol Ann's things but didn't find anything that would work for Molly until we started to go through Dick's clothing.

Even though there was only one candle in Carol Ann's room, I could see the frown on Molly's face.

"We'll find something better someday," I said.

"Sure," she said sounding absolutely and utterly defeated.

We went back to the fire to warm up. It felt like it took forever to get the chill out of my bones. And I was pretty sure it wasn't even completely out.

Molly and I spent the rest of the time we were awake by the fire. She didn't say anything for hours or what I assumed was hours.

I tried to get her to eat but it didn't work until I

convinced her it wasn't for her. It was for the baby because if he or she was okay, it would need the food. That had gotten to her and she finally started to eat albeit slowly.

I felt terrible for her. It was so bad that I couldn't even remember the last time I'd felt hungry. I forced myself to eat some kind of strawberry cereal bar but that was all I could stomach. It was difficult to accept that I couldn't just bring her to a doctor to get help... to get answers. The only thing we could do was to sit and wait.

Most of the time she kept her hand on her small stomach moving it in slow circles. It was as if she was hoping she'd feel something. I didn't know much about having children but I knew it would be months before she could feel anything. If she'd feel anything.

The bleeding had stopped almost as quickly as it had started. According to Molly, she'd stated after the episode that it hadn't been that much. A friend of hers had minor bleeding and still had a perfectly healthy baby nine months later.

It hadn't even been that long ago that Molly wasn't sure she wanted to bring a baby into this world but I could tell just how badly she wanted the baby. Maybe in a way, she needed the baby because if it were just her and I, she was ready to end it all.

At some point, Molly and I had fallen asleep. I wasn't sure how long I'd been asleep but for the first time in a very long time, I felt rested.

Molly was still lying there with her arms wrapped around her middle. There was a small frown on her face.

The fire had dwindled to nearly nothing. I threw a few pieces of wood in the fireplace and wrapped a blanket around my shoulders.

I sighed as I made my way over to the window. It felt like a waste of time to even check because I could feel it was still cold but it had become a habit.

When I pulled back the curtain, my hand shot up to my mouth. The blanket fell to my feet in a heavy whoosh.

I couldn't believe it. The world was a washed out gray. I could see the trees that surrounded us. The sun wasn't high in the sky relighting our world but I could tell it would rise.

Somehow, we'd made it through the darkness and the dawn was finally coming.

TWENTY-SEVEN

By the time I got Molly over to the window, the world was even brighter. The sun was rising just as it would any other morning.

I couldn't hear the ice rain falling but I could see it still frozen to everything outside. Once the clouds were completely gone and the sun warmed the earth, the ice would melt.

"Am I dreaming?" Molly asked.

"No," I said unable to stop a smile.

"It's still so cold," Molly said.

I nodded. "It'll take some time."

It was still too cold to be away from the fire for too long. Molly and I went back to sit by the fireplace but this time I left the curtain open. I wanted to watch the world light up again.

With each minute the outside light got brighter. And I became more and more hopeful.

Whoever was launching these attacks wasn't finished. Maybe they wouldn't ever be finished. Did they know people were still alive?

Somehow, I'd survived another but I knew that one of these times I wouldn't be so lucky because that's all it was... luck.

It had been several days before things started to warm up again. Our days had been long but calm. Each night when I went to bed, I worried that when I opened my eyes again, the darkness would be back and that the sunlight returning would have only been a dream.

The ice that had coated everything was melting. There must have been a thick layer on the room because water streamed down the windows relentlessly. It looked like water was soaking in through the ceiling leaving behind water stains. Once the ice was off of the roof, I was almost certain the inside of the house would start to warm up.

It had been exactly three days after the sun had returned that I started watching for Nick and Bronx. I wasn't sure when we could expect them to return but I hoped it would be soon. It was possible that they would wait for all of the ice to melt but maybe they were already on their way.

Molly had started eating normally again at some point although I didn't remember when. When I looked into her eyes, I could still see all the worry they held. I wondered if she'd been able to see it in mine even though I tried hard to hide it.

It was the fourth day when I couldn't pull myself away from the window. I wanted to see Nick and Bronx walking toward the house. It was roughly noon based on the position of the sun but there was still no sign of life besides myself and Molly.

Maybe we were all that was left. With all the silence that surrounded us that was exactly how it felt.

I was about to give up my watch when I heard something. A rustling. A twig cracking. The noise had been faint and distant but I knew I'd heard something.

"Molly," I whispered.

"Yeah?"

"Shh!"

She narrowed her eyes at me. "You're the one ta—"

"I heard something."

"It was probably just a squirrel."

I nodded but kept my voice low. "Probably. Where is Carol Ann's shotgun?"

"I don't know," Molly said shaking her head as she looked around. "Should we go hide? In the basement thingy?"

"Maybe," I said my eyes darting around trying to spot what had made the noise through the trees.

I placed my hand on the cold glass and sighed. Molly had probably been right... it had only been a....

My spine straightened. I saw the gate open and someone running as fast as they could toward the house. As far as I could tell he was alone. At least I thought it was a he.

His head was down and every third step the person tripped catching themselves with their hand. With the last stumble, the man rolled to the ground. When he looked up, I saw a bearded face that was covered in mud but the eyes... the eyes I knew.

"Nick!" I said almost stumbling myself as I dashed to the front door.

"What?" Molly said placing her hands on her belly as she took a step closer. It looked like she was about to cry. "Why did you say his name?"

"Because it's him. He's out there." I opened the front door just as Nick was approaching.

Nick took three large steps the last one placing

him inside of the house. He quickly but silently closed the door. His breathing was frantic and his eyes were filled with urgency.

"Go!" Nick said. "You have to go!"

"What are you talking about?" I asked.

"They're coming. You need to take Molly and get out of here. I'll slow them. I'll catch up." Nick sucked in a breath. "Just get out of here!"

I shook my head. "What's going on? Where's Bronx?"

"I don't have time to explain," Nick said.

"You need to. Talk fast," I urged.

Nick grabbed my arm and then Molly's as he led us to the back door. "Where's Christian? Carol Ann?"

"They... they didn't make it," Molly said.

"Bronx and I escaped from some very bad men. I imagine they are the people that Tom had warned us about." Nick looked over his shoulder as if he thought they were behind him. "They're coming. They're not far behind."

"We can hide in the basement," Molly said.

Nick shook his head. "They know about the basement. Dick is with them. He told them everything about this place right before they slit his throat."

"Where is Bronx?" I asked as I firmly planted my feet on the kitchen tile.

"I'm not sure," Nick said with a frown.

"What do you mean you're not sure?" I asked trying to keep my voice steady.

Nick looked away. "We got separated. He told me you'd know where to go. It's time to go there."

"Winnipeg?" I asked.

Nick nodded.

"Can we take anything?"

"A jacket. But then you need to go. Run and do not stop," Nick said.

Molly grabbed Nick's arm. "You have to come with us."

"I need to delay them so that you can get away." Nick looked into Molly's eyes before placing a kiss on her lips. He touched her belly and smiled. "You have to go. I love you. I love you both."

"Just come with us," I said shaking my head.

"I'll be right behind you," Nick said with a grin. He kissed Molly again. "I wasn't sure if I'd ever see you again. You're just as beautiful as I remember. You kept me going."

Nick coughed harshly covering his mouth with his hand. When he pulled it back, I saw a bit of blood on his fingers. He tried to hide it but when he met my eyes, he knew I'd seen.

"Go," he said. "Take care of my baby." He turned to me and gave me a quick hug. "I'm sorry I was such a shitty brother but I have to ask one thing of you."

"What's that?" I asked.

"Take care of Molly," Nick said.

"I will," I said biting my cheek in an attempt not to burst into tears.

Bronx was gone and I was pretty sure Nick had the poison... what was the point to continue? What was the point of running?

I pulled a jacket off of the hook and quickly slipped it on. Molly copied me and took down what looked to be one of Dick's old windbreakers. Neither of our coats would be warm enough if the darkness came back.

There were noises at the front door. I could hear people talking.

"Go!" Nick whispered. "Don't stop. Don't stop for anything."

"How will you find us?" Molly asked a tear trickling down her cheek.

"I know where you're going," Nick said. "Now, please, go!"

I grabbed Molly's arm and pulled her out the

back door just as someone burst in through the front. Nick grabbed a knife from the knife block on the counter and ducked down.

I could hear them moving around the house. It sounded like a herd of elephants had been released inside the home.

I kept pulling Molly along, tightening my grip when I heard stomping and shouting. The kitchen table squeaked as it moved across the floor.

"Get him! He's the one that got away!" someone shouted. They'd found him.

TWENTY-EIGHT

"We have to go back and help him!" Molly said trying to pull herself away from me.

"There's nothing we can do for him," I said, my voice cracking. "There are too many of them."

I could see them in the window. We were drastically outnumbered and it sounded like more and more were filling the space with each passing second.

"He's sick," I said and Molly's arm went limp. "I saw the blood when he coughed."

"That doesn't mean anything," Molly said. "He made it all the way here. He's fighting it off."

A gunshot cut through the air followed by a laugh. It felt like a blade had sliced through my chest and into a part of my heart.

"Come on," I said.

"No," Molly cried covering her mouth to muffle the sounds.

Her shoulders shook uncontrollably but I kept pulling her along. If I didn't guide her, she would have dropped to her knees and curled up into a ball letting her emotions take over.

I bit my cheek so hard I'd cut through the skin. The metallic taste filled my mouth almost causing me to gag.

I couldn't believe he was gone. He had been a terrible brother in the past but when it came down to it, he was the reason we were alive. He'd protected us. He'd taken care of us. In my eyes, he'd made up for everything. I only wished I could have told him.

My shoulders slumped and the corners of my eyes filled up with wetness. The tear that dripped out and rolled down my cheek landed on my lips letting a faint saltiness into my mouth.

My knees were weak but I had to force myself to keep going. Nick had stayed back, so that they didn't know they'd be looking for others. He'd saved us... one... last... time.

We were just about to step out of the trees and into a clearing when I heard whispering. Two men stepped out each from behind a tree. They grinned at us as if they'd found their dinner.

"Well, look at what we found," one of the men said.

The one closest to Molly moved quickly, grabbing her arm roughly. He pulled her away from me with a jerk that almost caused her to lose her balance.

Molly clawed at his hand and when that didn't work, she tried to scratch his face. He didn't look happy but he didn't let go.

The other man moved quickly... he was coming for me. He bared his teeth like a wild animal as he reached out for me.

I twisted to the side just out of his reach. He growled as he pivoted and reached out of me again. This time he got hold of my jacket and pulled me back toward him.

I slammed into his body but bent my arm and jerked my elbow back into his face. He howled when I connected with his nose.

"Bitch!" he screeched.

I didn't stop. I sucked in a breath as I grabbed his shoulder and rammed my knee as hard as I could between his legs.

The man dropped to the ground and I kicked him in the stomach. He reached out for my leg as blood poured out of his nose plopping big, red drops onto the wet ground. When he caught my ankle, I shifted my balance to the foot he was holding and kicked him in the face with my other.

For a second, murderous rage filled his eyes but then they rolled back into his head and his hand dropped away from me. I'd managed to knock him out.

"You're going to be sorry for that!" the other man said grabbing Molly tighter.

I held up my fists and he pulled her back to him with a roar. The man kept his eyes on me... waiting nervously for my next move.

"Let her go," I demanded.

He laughed.

"Okay, you asked for it," I said launching myself toward him.

Before he could let go of Molly to protect his face, I popped him just under his eye. Molly pushed him away as she broke free of his grip.

"Hit him again!" Molly said.

I pulled my fist back but before I was able to hit him, he held out his palms and pushed my shoulders. I fell backward landing on my bottom.

He smiled as he came closer. The man reached down grabbing the front of my jacket.

"You're not going to like what I'm about to do to you," he said.

"Arrr!" Molly shouted as she jumped onto his back.

The man didn't let go as he fell to the side with Molly still on top of him. Her hands moved quickly as she attacked him.

With one quick movement, he swept her off of him as if she were nothing more than a pesky mosquito. He rolled on top of me, raising his fist.

"I'm going to enjoy this," he said.

"No," a voice said. "I'm going to enjoy this."

A loud bang filled the air and blood showered down on top of me. The man's eyes emptied and he rolled to his side.

Nick was standing there. Looking down at us. "Looked like you had that under control."

"Wh— what are you doing here?" I asked as if I wasn't sure if he were real.

"Told you I'd catch up," he said. Nick stretched out his hand to Molly and then to me. "We need to get moving. I thought you two would have made it further than this."

"Aren't they back there?" I asked.

"They are," Nick said. "I've delayed them, just like I said I would."

I shook my head. "I heard a gunshot."

"Yeah and I'm sure they heard that one," Nick said. "They'll come to investigate."

He motioned for us to move and Molly and I followed him. We ran... we ran like the devil himself was chasing us.

"I thought you were dead?" I said between breaths.

"I thought I was going to be too but I shot one of his men... one of his important men. Then I knocked over that lantern. They were more concerned with stopping the fire than they were to catch me," Nick said raising a brow as if he were proud of himself.

I swallowed hard and looked back over my shoulder. "Will they come after us?"

"Maybe... probably," Nick said. "That's why we have to move quickly. Leave no trace but they have someone that can track."

"Track?" Molly asked.

"Yeah," Nick said. "He's very good. We just have to hope they'll be happy with the house and leave us alone."

I drew in a breath. "Is that likely?"

"I don't know. These men... they're bad," Nick said. "I'm lucky to be alive."

"Is Bronx—"

"He's not dead. I told you he got away but that we got separated." Nick wouldn't look in my direction. "He told me what you two had talked about. That's where he'll go. He knew the men were going for the house. He'll be there."

I looked back again hoping I'd see him running after us. When he wasn't there, I bit my cheek again in the same spot I'd already broken the skin.

I couldn't cry.

Not now.

Not until we were safe.

Nick looked at me. "He'll be there."

"Yeah," I said tasting my blood.

"We were prisoners," Nick said. "Carol Ann's stupid map led us right to them."

"Did she know?" I asked.

He shook his head. "I don't think she did. It sounded like they had only recently taken over the area. Dick was being held against his will too."

We'd probably ran at least a mile before Nick slowed slightly. He looked behind us and drew in a breath.

"They found out about his house. He'd said something. He tried to protect Carol Ann for as long as he could." Nick frowned. "They promised no harm would come to her as long as he told them where the house was. He told them and they killed him. I knew I had to get away... warn you."

"And you did." Molly smiled.

"Unfortunately, I had to go out into the freezing ice crap," he said with a cough. This time when I looked at his hand his fingers didn't have any fresh blood on them.

Molly looked at him and blinked. "You're sick?"

"I'm fighting it off," Nick said. "At least I'm trying to."

"You will," I said confidently. "Christian and Carol Ann were both gone rather quickly. You're still here. That's a good sign."

Nick nodded. "I hope you're right, Sis. With the others I saw get sick, it was the same. They vomited out their insides and then they were gone. That didn't happen to me. At least not to the same level."

"Good," I said.

"It is," he said waving us along. "Let's keep moving. We've got a long walk ahead of us."

I couldn't resist taking one last look over my shoulder. There wasn't anyone chasing us. And there was no Bronx.

TWENTY-NINE

After miles and miles of walking, we finally found a gas station. The entire building had a dreadful stench of rot and decay. I was almost certain if we walked into the back offices, we'd find at least one corpse.

We didn't go into the back.

There wasn't much left in the way of supplies throughout the gas station but there was enough food that had been left behind to take the edge off of our hunger.

On the wall at the back of the room near the restrooms was a bulletin board. There were faded signs and business cards pinned to the board along with a map that indicated our exact location. We could see just how much further we had to go to make it to Winnipeg and to say the least, it looked daunting. It was a long way to go.

"I'm going to have to find another pair of shoes," I said swallowing as I looked away from the map. The treads on the ones I was wearing were already worn down.

"We'll find some," Nick said. "You know what we really need?"

Molly shook her head.

"What?" I asked.

"Horses," Nick said with a raised brow.

I stared at him for a moment trying to decide if he was serious. It seemed as though he was.

I chose not to address the fact that we hadn't seen many animals. They too were suffering from the effects of the attacks.

There was a part of me that was hopeful about our future. I thought that we'd make it and once we did, Bronx would be there waiting for us. He'd wave and smile.

But there was another part of me that was more realistic. I knew traveling to Winnipeg was just a task that would keep us busy until the next attack that would probably take our lives once and for all.

Molly and Nick hadn't let go of each other since we'd left Carol Ann's house. It was hard to watch them but I couldn't blame them. If I ever saw Bronx again, which deep down I didn't think I would, I wouldn't let go of him either.

I should have done more to stop him from leaving in the first place. It was partially my fault that he was gone. If I would have begged him to stay, he probably would have.

Nick had said he'd seen Bronx running away. The last time he'd seen him, he'd been alive... that was what I needed to hold on to. That one tiny glimmer of hope that he was out there looking for me.

It was frustrating that we were back to where we started. We had no food, no water and no supplies. At least we had the shotgun even though I was afraid to ask how many shots were left or if he'd managed to grab any ammo on his way out of Carol Ann's home. Something told me he hadn't.

I told myself that if we did it once we could do it again. Supplies might be dwindling but so were people. Competition for what remained was less and less with each attack.

"I think we should rest here for the night," Nick said.

"But it smells so bad here," Molly said pinching her nostrils together.

I looked out of the window. "What if they're behind us?"

"They're noisy. We'll hear them coming a mile away," Nick said. "The whole lot of them are over-confident with everything they do. They think they're invincible."

"You're not afraid of them?" Molly asked.

"Nah," Nick said but then laughed at himself. "I'm terrified of them. They're like cavemen. They don't give a shit about anything or anyone."

I dragged my index finger across my dry lower lip. "Then maybe we should keep going. We need to put in as many miles as we can before the next attack."

"My leg needs the rest," Nick said.

"Oh, sure, yeah. No problem," I said staring at his leg. It looked perfectly fine but I could still remember the moment he'd been shot.

I wondered if Winnipeg would have a doctor. Not that there was much they could probably do for Nick but Molly would need care.

I stayed at the window while Nick and Molly spent some time together. They kept their voices quiet and stayed out of sight.

Outside the window, ice still covered parts of the

ground. There were deep puddles were some of the ice had started to melt during the day.

Feeling the sunlight on my skin had been nearly life-changing. I wanted to believe that the light was a sign that things were going to be good. Better.

But that was a hard, if not impossible, thing to allow myself to believe. After everything we'd been through, it felt like things were only getting worse and worse.

It would be night soon and I wouldn't admit it to a soul but I was afraid of the coming darkness. We wouldn't have a candle or a flashlight but worst of all I would fear that the sun wouldn't rise again in the morning.

At least with the big purple storm cloud gone, I'd hope the moon would light the night sky. The sun reflecting on its surface would remind me that it was still there.

Watching the sun go down hadn't been anywhere near as beautiful as watching it rise had been. I tried to fight away my panic... reminding myself repeatedly that the attack was over and the darkness would only be temporary.

I wasn't sure how long I'd sat in the increasing darkness before someone lightly touched my shoulder. My whole body jerked at the touch. I looked over my shoulder barely relaxing when I saw Nick standing behind me.

"Hey," he said softly, looking at me as if it were the first time he was seeing me.

"Hi," I said squinting at him.

Nick let out a breath and wrapped his arms around me. It was a quick hug but it was filled with something I wasn't sure I'd ever felt from Nick before. A feeling I wasn't even sure how to describe... Love? Fear? It was a combination of many things but it was oddly comforting.

"I wasn't sure if I'd ever see you again," Nick said. "I hadn't felt that way since I was making my way to your apartment after the first attack."

My throat instantly felt dry. I wasn't exactly sure what to say. I wanted to tell him how stupid it had been to go out on his own but I knew he had his reasons. And he thought he was doing it for me, Molly and his unborn baby.

"I know I've been a terrible brother over the years but I'm going to change that."

"It's not like I've been that great of a sister," I said with a small shrug. I'd never forgiven him. I probably blamed him for far much more than I should have about a lot of things... mainly our mother.

"You have been." Nick took a step back and

crossed his arms. "Molly told me you know about the baby."

"I do. Congratulations."

"You don't sound like you mean that."

I swallowed hard. "I do, but I worry, you know? This isn't an easy life."

His head bobbed up and down as he stared in Molly's direction. I followed his gaze seeing her fast asleep on the floor in a rather uncomfortable position.

"She doesn't seem like herself," Nick said.

"Well, it's a lot for her to take in. I mean, who would want to be pregnant with all this going on? No doctors. She's probably scared out of her mind," I said.

"Yeah... yeah. I'm sure that's what it is," Nick said.

It didn't seem as though Molly had mentioned the bleeding episode to Nick. Perhaps that was why he was getting a strange vibe from her. If he would have known he would have likely been more worried himself.

"She missed you terribly," I said. "Things got pretty low for a while."

"For me too," Nick admitted but I didn't think he could guess how close Molly had been to walking out into the falling poison ice. "I'm afraid to think what would have happened if you hadn't been there."

I shook my head. "I didn't do anything special."

"You took care of her. You're always taking care of everyone."

"Oh, please. I can barely take care of myself," I said waving my hand in the air.

Nick chuckled. "That's because you're too busy tending to everyone else's needs."

"You give me far too much credit."

"One day you'll see what I see," Nick said. "And what everyone else sees. Hell, you were an animal fighting those guys off back there. Who taught you to fight like that?"

I laughed. "You were the one that did all the work, pulling out your gun."

"Aw come on, Sis. You didn't need my help," Nick said. "Anyway." He looked down at his feet and then back into my eyes. "I'm proud of you. We're all lucky to have you on our side."

"Thanks," I said not wanting to discuss it any further. I could accept his compliment but that didn't mean I had to believe them.

"Want me to take watch for a while?" Nick asked.

I swallowed hard. I didn't want to miss Bronx if

he happened to wander by. Of course, I knew how unlikely that was but that didn't matter.

"You know we're going to find him, right?" Nick said. "He's out there right now fighting his way back to you. That man loves you."

I looked away. Imagining my life without Bronx wasn't something I was ready to do. Nor was it something I wanted to do. Especially since we had so many miles ahead of us.

Maybe it would be better if I just pretended to be the person Nick thought I was. It wouldn't hurt anything and really what choice did I have?

It felt like it had been a different life but I'd made a promise to Bronx that I would keep going no matter what.

We had to keep going. We had to find Winnipeg. If there was anyone that could make it there... it was us.

BOOKS BY KELLEE L. GREENE

Red Sky Series

Red Sky - Book 1

Blue Cloud - Book 2

Black Rain - Book 3

White Dust - Book 4

Indigo Ice - Book 5

Book 6 Coming Soon!

Ravaged Land Series

Ravaged Land -Book 1

Finding Home - Book 2

Crashing Down - Book 3

Running Away - Book 4

Escaping Fear - Book 5

Fighting Back - Book 6

Ravaged Land: Divided Series

The Last Disaster - Book 1

The Last Remnants - Book 2

The Last Struggle - Book 3

Falling Darkness Series

Unholy - Book 1

Uprising - Book 2

Hunted - Book 3

The Island Series

The Island - Book 1

The Fight - Book 2

The Escape - Book 3

The Erased - Book 4

The Alien Invasion Series

The Landing - Book 1

The Aftermath - Book 2

Destined Realms Series

Destined - Book 1

MAILING LIST

Sign up for Kellee L. Greene's mailing list for new releases, sales, cover reveals and more!

Sign up: http://eepurl.com/bJLmrL

You can Find Kellee on Facebook:

www.facebook.com/kelleelgreene

ABOUT THE AUTHOR

Kellee L. Greene is a stay-at-home-mom to two super awesome and wonderfully sassy children. She loves to read, draw and spend time with her family when she's not writing. Writing and having people read her books has been a long time dream of hers and she's excited to write more. Her favorites genres are Fantasy and Sci-fi. Kellee lives in Wisconsin with her husband, two kids and two cats.

For more information:
www.kelleelgreene.com

facebook.com/kelleelgreene

twitter.com/kelleelgreene

Made in the USA
Coppell, TX
16 August 2021